An Algarve Affair

Janice Russell, PhD, was born in seventeen to study for her first degree in Sociology. She subsequently acquired three postgraduate degrees, including her MA in Creative Writing, while being a full-time mum. Janice has worked extensively across many cultures, coaching, teaching, developing and writing. She has lived part-time and sometimes full-time in the Algarve since 2000.

More books from Janice Russell:

Fiction

Keeping Abreast (1998) Insight Press
A Waste of Good Weather (2013) Insight Press

Non Fiction

Out of Bounds (1994) London: Sage
Blank Minds and Sticky Moments in Counselling (1998, 2008) London: Sage
An Introduction to Coaching (2011) London: Sage

An Algarve Affair

Janice Russell

MONTANHA
BOOKS

An Algarve Affair

Published by Insight Press in association with
Montanha Books
Apt 8, Monchique 8550-909, Algarve, Portugal
www.montanhabooks.com
Contact: info@montanhabooks.com

ISBN: 978-0-9515525-6-8

Typeset in point 11.5 Times New Roman

Cover image by Suzi Steinhofel
www.suzisteinhofel.com

For all of my good time friends along the way, with special mention to Lady Svahn of Little Brington, rising, and Rachel Ward, who will recognise some Oxford cameos, and, more hilariously, holds the secret of the garment. I am glad you are in my life.

a funny thing has happened to me on the way to the Algarve

april 1st 2010

'Bitch.' Henry smoothed an eyebrow with his forefinger as he looked me full in the face.

I bristled, drew myself up.

'I beg your pardon?'

'I said, you're a bit of a bitch,' declared Henry. 'And what's more, you're quite blatantly a Fattist.'

He chuckled, audaciously.

'Well, not really a Fattist, Henry, it's just that…'

'Which is not good coming f-from a woman who claims a degree of expertise in diversity training.'

He brushed at his Kindle to turn a page, drawing a line. Subject closed. I seethed, making a mental note to raise this incident with Fenella, my life coach. I bit carefully into a square of bacon dipped in egg yolk and reviewed the events which had led to Henry's spiteful accusation.

The day was barely dawning when I was bundled into a taxi at six o'sodding clock this morning, embarking on the first leg of my surprise holiday, a gift from my accuser. Surprises are tricky, aren't they, you don't know what to pack. I hedged my bets with layers, chucked in walking boots, a rainproof, bikini, and a selection of undies including my Agent Provocateur set complete with suspenders for wildest scenario.

I gathered that wildest scenario was unlikely as soon as Henry told the taxi driver 'East Midlands Airport'. Not many long haul flights from EMA, and while there are plenty of places in Europe where decadence features high, EMA has a certain prudent and practical aspect about it. Budget airlines, good value.

Very Henry.

More prudent than provocative.

Once at Departures. Henry put our luggage on a trolley and proudly ushered me toward the Ryanair check-in. Our choices narrowed, Malaga or Faro.

We joined the queue for Faro. Henry was taking me to the Algarve!

So far so good. The Algarve's quite gauche in its way, I gather. Dishy Dragon Peter Jones stays there, probably drinking

7

wine matured from Sir Cliff's vineyard. Monica Ali wrote a book in that region I think, and loads of sports personalities and TV chefs hang out there, not to mention Madonna. So it must have something going for it.

And I *was* relieved it wasn't Malaga.

Once checked in, Henry went to order breakfast, and I went to WHSmith's to get a magazine or two.

Which is where events got complicated.

I quickly perused the gossip mags, then zoomed in on Health and Beauty, seeking the correct journal to make me feel better and trimmer if I read it while eating breakfast. *Rosemary Conley* magazine promised two inches off my waist in a fortnight if I followed her diet and exercise regime.

While I was looking through it, a woman approached me. She was plump, shorter than me, with probably a similar amount of wear and tear.

'Excuse me,' she said, in a north Midlands accent, 'could I just get past?'

'Of course,' I said. I thought she wanted Health and Beauty as well, that she would be in search of some serious self-help.

Wrong. She went instead for *Hello* magazine, *She*, and an issue of *Cosmo* with a cellophane cover, applied to entrap a centrefold of full frontal male nudes. Then, she did no more than to go to the chocolate stall and buy three of those small bags of Thornton continentals. *Three.* Clearly more motivated by pleasure than self-discipline – *pure* pleasure, not balanced or negotiated, not put in place as a reward for achieving a well earned goal, but spontaneous, unadulterated indulgence.

Wow.

D'you know, I can't remember the last time I did the same.

I had a violent temptation to buy a whole box of Thornton's. Instead, I grabbed hold of and paid for the Rosemary Conley mag, complete with its allure of a sleek and super fit body.

So when I got to the café to meet Henry, magazine safely in hand, I was slightly flummoxed. I blurted out the story of the Thornton's Tart as I picked at my high protein breakfast.

'I nearly succumbed,' I confessed, 'but that kind of indulgence does take its toll. She had bulges under the bra strap in abundance.'

It was then that Henry made the accusation about me being a Fattist.

I couldn't help but wonder whether Henry has a point? Here was I, Lecturer in English and Women's Studies for a recently upgraded University college, Equality and Diversity rep on the college board, and I was bleating on about bulges under the bra strap.

A morsel of egg yolk plopped from my fork onto my lapel. I erased it with my finger, but it left a nasty smear.

I suddenly felt tearful. Was he right? In one way, of course he's right. I fight tooth and nail for people to be equally valued, and yet I just don't find fat attractive, particularly on myself.

I ruminated on the philosophical implications.

If a woman goes inside her mind and has prejudiced thoughts, but no one is around to hear or police them, and she never acts on them except in relation to herself, are they still prejudiced?

And if she discloses her sad inner turmoil to a confidante, but doesn't treat fat people badly, is she really a Fattist?

I put down my knife and fork, my appetite swallowed up by my ruminations.

Breakfast discarded, we had thirty minutes until boarding, so went our separate ways, me to Duty Free, Henry to Dixons. I explored all the goodies on show, splashed out on some Estée Lauder and bought a large flagon of water.

And then a second disconcerting thing happened.

I was just leaving Duty Free, when I *saw* the aforementioned fitness guru Rosemary Conley, sitting at a table at the edge of Wetherspoon's. I did a double take, wondering if my disturbed mind was playing tricks on me. But it was definitely her.

Serendipity or what.

There she was, large as life (in a slim kind of way), slumming it with a black coffee at seven o'clock in the morning. *Rosemary Conley*, the epitome of a woman in control of herself: not just a pretty face, but entrepreneur extraordinaire, sitting on a multimillion pound empire full of magazines, DVDs, apps.

Rosemary Conley turns fat into cash.

She looked brilliant, just brilliant. She was wearing a short calfskin jacket, black crop trousers, and trimly cut hair – not a glob of fat to be seen.

And I searched, believe me, I *scrutinized*.

I backed off when she raised an eyebrow at me after I circled the Wetherspoon's bar for the second time, doing my best to keep my gaze surreptitious. She said something to the young guy sitting next to her, then looked at me as if to say, 'Do I know you?' Or maybe she was thinking, 'Wow, look at the bingo wings on her.' I suppose she might even have been thinking, 'What the fuck are you staring at?'

I smiled and gave a convivial nod, as if to let her know she was my kind of Fattist, and walked away, making it clear that I would not be stalking her.

I waited till I was a reasonable distance before I got her photo on my phone.

When the flight was announced, I crammed my purchases into my handbag, my handbag into my hand luggage, and made my way toward the gate. Henry waved from the front of Priority Boarding, and once under starter's orders, dipped his hand luggage swiftly in and out of the size checker before leading the charge to the plane. By the time I boarded, he was waving to me from the extra leg room seats near the front of the plane.

As we settled into our economy seats with our non-economy leg room, I told him about seeing RC.

'You'd never know her age,' I said to Henry, 'if you didn't look at her hands. They really are the only give away – usually it's neck as well, but she's very well preserved in that region. *And* she was with a much younger man, only twenty-nine or thirty, so she's obviously done all right for herself, because she must be fifty-five if she's a day.'

'Heavens,' said Henry, positioning his Kindle carefully in the seat pocket, and unpacking his travel outfit of eye mask, ear plugs, neck pillow and body wipes. He patted my knee. 'Heavens.'

The pilot was talking about going to Alicante and everyone laughed. Initially I found this alarming – was the man drunk, or what – but Henry said it was just great that the pilot had a sense of humour, and wondered who he'd been trained by. Henry is a Training Director for **Go4It**, his father's business, and the company has just got the training contract with another airline, as it happens. So Henry made a little note on his Blackberry before blowing up his neck pillow, putting on the eye mask, slotting in the earplugs, and falling immediately into a contented sleep.

I took out my compact and looked closely at my face. It seemed to have lost hydration by the very act of getting on the plane. I applied Estée Lauder's Eight Hour Cream, and took a large sip of water. I checked my lip-gloss, and I looked around.

No sign of RC.

Instead, an array of more or less engaging sights. Ahead, a woman had slipped off her shoes and was wiggling her toes inside comfy looking slouch socks. Two women were clambering past her, one sporting purple and lime green florals, the other a black and white hooped dress through which you could see the outline of her panties. A man a few rows down was reaching up to put away his hand luggage, his big belly escaping over a waistband which had emigrated to his hips. In the row directly across the aisle sat a Portuguese couple, immaculately groomed, sporting gold on their fingers, wrists and necks, their linen slacks sitting well on their well preserved, or well corseted, bottoms. Here and there babies and small children whimpered, screeched or chattered, patient parents soothed and fussed.

I settled back with my magazine, uttered a hasty prayer, and tried to relax while the plane took off. I don't believe in God, but I have a word with her now and then just in case. It seems to have worked so far.

Once in the air, I welcomed the release of the cabin crew and the calming voice of the stewardess which reverberated around the metal tube in which I was being propelled at speed through the sky.

'Ladies and gentlemen, the seat belt signs are still on, please keep them fastened until the captain sees fit to turn the sign off. Then you will be free to leave your seats and search around the plane to see if you would like to sit by someone more attractive. Smoking is strictly prohibited on the plane, and anyone found smoking will be asked to leave immediately.'

The whole plane tittered. Despite it being a jocular announcement, the comment about sitting by someone more attractive caused me to stop and look at Henry *vis à vis* the attractiveness stakes.

Because of his traveller's eye mask, it was difficult to make a full appraisal. It's also true that when people are sleeping while sitting upright, their mouths and jaws don't always fall at a favourable angle: this slight snag apart, Henry came out quite well. A little pale perhaps, a sign of too much time at the office, and there is the odd wrinkle round the eyes and neck. But by and large he has a nice shaped face, a distinguished brow, and lovely dark hair with only the slightest hint of grey, just where it should be, around the temples and the sideburns. Shell shaped ears, the one nearest to me sporting a tiny hole, which these days hardly ever sees an earring, what with office protocol and so on: but I like the fact that he's had this much rebellion in him at one time at least.

I smiled fondly. Henry is definitely one of my more discerning life choices.

Next thing I knew, the cabin staff were on their way with the refreshments trolley. I bought a cup of tea, resisting the selection of snacks. I did what Fenella has taught me – instead of just grabbing for what I want, I imagined how my stomach would feel one hour after eating, and decided that a box of Pringles or giant Mars bar might sit too heavily. I wished I'd remembered to pop some dried apricots or something into my bag, as I was quite peckish again already. Half a bacon rasher didn't last long.

Then I heard someone behind me.

'Cheese and pickle sandwich, red wine and a large chunky Kit Kat, please.'

I knew I recognised the voice, but couldn't recall where from. I turned my head and peeked behind, and blow me, if it wasn't the treacherous Thornton's Tart from the Smith's counter. I must say that she looked very well on it all, her plumpness giving a soft complexion to her face, and even her lines seemed smiley. I tried to make a real conscious effort to remind myself what poor eating habits do to your insides, and to resist, for the second time today, acting on a powerful attack of envy.

But I didn't succeed. Instead, I called the stewardess back, and ordered myself a small bottle of bubbly and a giant packet of Maltesers, and immediately felt much better. Henry murmured gently in his sleep.

Once I'd had a sip and a nibble, I got Henry's laptop out of his bag under the seat, put on headphones, and had a mooch through his films. Henry's heavily into films, and his collection ranges from classics such as *Calamity Jane* through to more recent stuff, like *The Girl with the Dragon Tattoo,* pirate original. I fancied something light but fun. I opted for *Bridget Jones.* I use the book in my English classes with the adult returners, but haven't watched the film for ages. There are rumours that Helen Fielding is in talks about producing a third one next year. Anyway, I reckoned it would be just right to entertain me for the main part of the journey.

But, to my surprise, the film grated.

Although it's witty in parts, and poignant, the film definitely lacks the depth of the book. I started getting irritated. Why had there been all that hype around Renée Zellweger having to put on weight for the role? Didn't she once claim after the first movie that her arse was the size of Brazil? Well if that's so, mine must be the size of Australia plus some. Quite frankly, the woman doesn't know what she's on about.

And Henry calls *me* Fattist!

I took another handful of Maltesers.

To be honest, as I washed them down with my champagne, I realised that I am more than a little pissed off with the compulsive self-obsession that goes with so called girl power this last decade or two. Thirty-somethings, really, what are they like, whingeing about being *single*, and how *difficult* it is and how there might be a *wrinkle* coming. They need to get over themselves: at least they're not plucking stray eyebrows out of their chins.

Truth is, when young, smooth-faced women complain about ageing, I increasingly want to grab hold of a pair of tweezers and poke them in the eyes.

Is that normal, do you think?

I ordered a second bottle of bubbly. I left the film running, and pondered, surprised by my lack of equilibrium. Then I thought, what is there to read about what happens *after* thirty-something, about what happens when we're forty-something, even nearly fifty-something, sixty-something and beyond? I couldn't think of much off hand.

So do people imagine that if us post-thirty-somethings aren't boot camped and botoxed half to death, we simply reach for slippers and Zimmer frames and take up crochet or hill walking? Should we take out a subscription to silver-surfers-r-us.com and sit down and wait to die?

Sod that for a lark.

I gulped more champagne.

It strikes me that there's a lot more to the 'ordinary' woman than meets the commercial eye. My generation is the tail end of the baby boomers. We *invented* rock music, embodied the spirit of free love, abandoned our bras, and only got out of our heads in a recreational sort of way. We camped out at Greenham Common to protest against nuclear arms, did sit ins in universities all over the world, took to the streets against racism and sexism, rediscovered Simone de Beauvoir and Betty Friedan, argued over the radical feminism of Andrea Dworkin, set up housing co-ops left right and centre, and fought for a woman's right to choose.

And for what? Real feminism seems to have been subsumed in a culture featuring fashion for stick insects clad in shoes more suited to whoring or stiletto warfare than to safe transportation down a cobbled street on a Saturday night.

It has become a mere rumble, audible only in carefully selected quarters. While women like Karen Brady are doing wonderful things in business, Sharon Osbourne's doctored face and body still command the envy of millions. Rates of personal anti ageing surgery have never been so high. Meanwhile, according to Tina Turner, seventy is the new fifty, and magazines tell us that, hair wise, grey is the new black.

Mixed messages. And I'm not sure where we are creating opportunities for *real* women to celebrate and use all that wisdom gained from previous cycles of feminism and sexual liberation.

I sighed, took another gulp of my bubbly, found myself determining that I'll draw on my own wisdom to at least preclude a mid-life crisis.

What else could I do?

By the time we landed early afternoon at Faro airport, I couldn't seem to stop my thoughts racing. Not when Henry and I disembarked into the soft warm air of the Algarve, nor as we marvelled at the clear open spaces as Henry drove us the hour's journey to our villa, him pointing and declaring at all and sundry – 'look, Izzie, there's a kind of a castle over there', 'is that a windmill?', 'look how blue the sky is', 'look, more pottery shops'; not even when we arrived in our lovely fishing village and toured the little cobbled streets, caught the salty taste of the deep blue sparkling sea on the afternoon air, smiled at the men in the pork pie hats that were sitting at the bus stop.

We found our villa fairly easily, just outside the main drag, and unpacked our bags. Spacious bedrooms housed spacious wardrobes.

'I guess I won't be needing this, then.'

Henry looked over as I hung my rain proof.

'Maybe more of that?'

He smiled as I carefully laid the Agent Provocateur underwear into a drawer. I gave him a hug.

'This is fab, Henry. I couldn't think of a better place to come to start my sabbatical.'

Henry beamed.

We heard a shout from downstairs, went to the balcony and looked down to the garden. We saw two guys standing there, one looking up, one walking down to the pool house.

'Pool men,' the one shouted, and Henry went down to say hello. When he came back up, he reported that they'd be coming twice a week to sweep out the leaves and all those sad little spiders and insects who find a watery grave.

'Seemed nice,' he said. 'And apparently there'll be maids coming too.'

Maids. Very colonial.

Once unpacked, we drove to a little supermarket called Ecomarché, for provisions. We bought essentials and desirables, and once we got back we went out on the sunbeds with a sandwich and a coffee and lay and relaxed.

Well, actually, I was still buzzing.

We decided to stay in for the first night. We showered and changed, made prawns and feta salad, drank a little red wine, meandered around various subjects. Then we had a post-prandial gin and tonic on the patio.

'D'you like it, sweetheart?' Henry gestured to the clear starry sky, taking in the sounds of the crickets and the frogs whose music added to the perfect ambience.

'I love it.' I chinked at Henry's glass.

'A whole month, Izzie, doing just exactly what you want. You don't need to do any work, you can mooch around to your heart's content, find out a bit more about the culture.' He downed his drink. 'And you can go and practise your diversity knowledge, but let's just hope that none of the Portuguese you meet are fat!'

Chuckling anew, Henry stood up.

'Actually, Henry, I have an idea.'

Henry bent and kissed me on the forehead.

'Well I'm very pleased, but right now, I have to go to bed, so I'll see you when you come up, or in the morning.'

And he was gone.

So I never got to tell him that my idea was to blog this month in the Algarve, the month in which I reach my half century. Fenella's suggested something similar before. She reckons that a journal is an invaluable aid to motivation and to achieving what we want. I'd never fancied it before, yet suddenly it seemed right to document a bit of life as a woman of my generation.

After all, we deserve a bit of recognition for all that we've made possible. .

And it will prove that I'm *not* a Fattist.

So here I am, registered on my Blogger. And look, I've done the whole of the first post.

Bed next, with a chamomile tea. Looking forward to a fantastic month ahead. Who knows how I'll come out at the other end of it. Comfortable in my skin I hope, refreshed and affirmed, at a stretch maybe even learning to grow older gracefully, still kicking but not screaming quite so much as I am prone to do.

And *definitely* full of champagne!

moi

april 2nd 2010

Despite my busy head, I had a good night's sleep. This morning I used some lavender eye bags, which are fab, and I've already done a bit of yoga on the terrace. Then I had to, or *chose* to, rather, given that my generation *invented* the new psychologies of empowerment, take a cup of tea up to dear old Henry. He's not an early riser, though I am. Early to bed, early to rise, makes you healthy, wealthy and wise, Attila (my mother) says. I'm sure she's right (even though she lives in a council house, just being renamed social housing, can you believe, and suffers a bit with irritable bowel syndrome, but at least no one can say that this is because she didn't get up early in the mornings).

I took the tea up to Henry, feeling perky and hoping to seduce him. He seems exceptionally tired from travelling. He took the cup and drank its contents in a somnambulant way. Tea dribbling down a chin is never a great aphrodisiac, so that put paid to my ideas of early morning sex. Henry went back to his slumber and I came back down to the sitting room.

Which is where I'm now writing. The villa is lovely; you can probably imagine the kind. White walls and terracotta floor tiles, big patio doors on to the terrace and a good sized swimming pool in a walled garden, which is teeming with Algarvian flora, loads of pinks, purples, crimsons and blues. Beyond the garden is a road, and over the road huge fields unfurl, dotted with old white houses sporting red tiled roofs. There are some horses in the field directly opposite, and an ancient donkey, back like a bow, munching tiredly away. The horizon is only some two kilometres from here, and over its brow is the sea.

In fact, while I await evidence of a pulse from Henry, I'll get a photo taken and I'll upload it a bit later on to the blog.

I suppose I could put a picture of me, though I'm not sure I want to be publicly revealed – yet. Fenella once coached me on the art of self-presentation, and suggested that I might do a self-presentation exercise, considering those aspects of myself that impact people on first meeting. I thought it a ridiculous suggestion at the time (no offence, Fenella), but perhaps now's the time for a dabble.

So here goes.

What do people first see of me? Well, I'm tall, with short dark hair. I have good cheekbones and a few laughter lines, kept in check for years by having long hair which I used to scrape up high and tight, coaxing the wrinkles out. I had it cut recently when I heard that style referred to as an Essex face lift. Now I have the look of a broom head first thing in the morning, or, as Henry likes to say, the look of the freshly laid. Once washed and gelled, I'm told the style is fetching. My eyes are brown and are large. I'm attractive, not beautiful, not ugly.

I don't know about you, but I have Good Face Days and Bad Face Days. On Good Face Days, I get up and look at the topography of my face in the mirror and admire the huge areas of still soft skin defying the predicted effects of the lifestyle it has been subject to. It seems that my dermal organ has not got thinner because of my erstwhile smoking habit.

(Actually, I still keep cigarettes for an occasional treat. They're menthol, which are not only not so *bad* for you, but taste like they are positively *good* for you. Obviously, on my fiftieth birthday, I shall quit☺).

On Good Face Days, my addiction to sunshine and a bit of an edgy life seems just to have left me with a healthy glow and a few laughter lines here and there. These are the kind of days when youthful eyes look back at me from the mirror, and I feel like I'm still seventeen inside, everything ahead of me.

Bad Face Days are quite different. On these days, my face looks all squashed up by how I've slept, like a crumpled old duvet, and seems lacking in moisture to plump up the little pink cells. The edges of my mouth incline to the south. I see deep crows' feet around my eyes, and, underneath, bags which seem to have retained most of the previous night's dry white wine on a localised basis.

If only I could funnel it out via a straw, bottle it and put it on ice – the ultimate in recycling.

I bother about my looks, though I don't think I'm obsessive about them. I cleanse and tone (Clinique 3-Step programme), apply Clarins face-lift-in-a-bottle, and cover with Clarins moisture balance cream. All natural products. I like to think I'm taking care, 'because I'm worth it', as the advert goes.

I don't fixate on my weight. I'm body conscious, and as per previous disclosure, I'm not keen on fat globules hanging in abundance where fat globules were never meant to hang. Everyone knows the old adage that inside every fat girl is a thin girl waiting to get out. Well, I'm a bit bothered that outside every slim girl is a fat girl waiting to get in. That said, I'm proud to say that I don't know how much I weigh. I don't even possess a pair of scales. A simple tape measure does the trick just as well, if not better, and is easy to carry around. I just pop the tape in a handbag with an exercise band, and Bob's your uncle, Fanny's your aunt, I've got a portable fit kit that keeps me on track.

I have great legs, or so I'm told. I still get admiring looks and the odd wolf whistle. At one time I'd have been offended by a wolf whistle as a typical and degrading manifestation of the objectification of women: these days I welcome it as a sign that I'm pretty fit.

My corpulent self has weathered the birth of four children, the loss of a parent, a successful career, a few live-in partners, much travel around Europe, the rise and fall of the British Left Wing, and the exposure of democracy as a farcical front for autocracy. It's said that the universe only throws at you what it thinks you can handle, and there have been times when I fervently wished it didn't have such faith in me. But here I am, and as I've said to Fenella, I'm a great one for believing that what doesn't kill you makes you stronger.

So, first impact. What's in a name?

Quite a lot, in my case.

My full name is Isabella Janet Ethel Childs

I got Isabella because it sounded upper class and well to do. My family of origin are working class Brummies who are loud, uneducated, and salt of the earth. Attila had greater aspirations for me, and in the calligraphy of *Isabella* perhaps she saw the opportunity for her daughter to be a woman of elegant lines, who might enjoy a life more lyrical than her own.

If so, she might have had a point. I associate 'Isabella' now with a sense of flow, a kind of ethereal quality, dancing, expression, and so on. When I was younger, and everyone else was called Ann, Susan, Mary, or Linda, my name made me stand out a bit. I was often accused of being stuck up, and felt isolated by the accusation. I suppose the experience was character building, in its way. In fact, it probably inspired my passion to strive for equality of opportunity and to fight prejudice, because once you've experienced it, you think twice before dealing it out.

Which makes it all the more shameful when you *do* feel a tiny prejudice.

So I would imagine.

The name 'Janet' was common as muck at the time I was born, but actually it was bestowed on me, apparently, to evoke the qualities of the Roman god Janus. He had cropped up in a *Woman's Weekly* New Year horoscope special of Attila's. Janus had the ability to look both forwards and backwards and thus adopt a balanced and fair view in life. Which is a pretty handy attribute for right now, I suppose, on the metaphorical eve of my mid-century.

Now and then, my inner Janus abilities to see both sides of the argument can make it difficult to be decisive. Overall, though, I'd say that balance and fairness are pretty good values to have (although I can also see how it would be great occasionally to know precisely which side to come out on and just bloody well stay there).

Ethel. Ethel, Ethel, Ethel. Now there's an appellation and a half. Not for 'Ethel' the romantic effect associated with the modern penchant for retro names such as Charlie, Harry and Rose. No. Far from. It really is a name for old people – I mean *really* old people, from a different era. I was named Ethel after a maternal aunt who died in a horrible accident shortly before my birth. All I know is that it was to do with a lighted candle, a man, and a pair of curtains, and I got that from overhearing a conversation between Atilla and our neighbour, Phyllis. I have never been given the full and sordid details. Ethel has always felt like an unwanted ghost. 'You're just like your aunty Ethel,' Attila would say, or 'your poor dead aunty Ethel would be ashamed of you'.

But it could be worse. I mean, I heard about a couple in the Black Country who named their daughter Chlamydia. *Chlamydia.* And even when the Health Visitor told the parents what it meant, they just said, 'ahh, sounds great though, doesn't it?' and left the poor child to deal with it for the rest of her life.

I just hope that her surname wasn't Thrush.

Childs is quite a new name to me. When I reached forty, I had a name analysis done by a talented guy in Milton Keynes. He did it by distance so that it only cost me eighty-five instead of one hundred pounds. In name analysis, they equate each letter in your name with a number, and then relate them all to each other on a mathematical basis. Quite scientific, apparently.

Then they relate each number to a significant portent and can tell you if your name is propitious or not. There's a Facebook version out now, where you can get an adjective equated with each letter, less scientific and more commercial, I would think.

My previous surname was Malleen. Turns out that although the sequence of two 'e's' together *can* mean good energy, in overabundance it indicates that you are accident prone, particularly to falls and tumbles. It looked like if I kept that name, I would be courting danger throughout the next five years, which was the last thing I wanted. So I chose Childs because then I could keep the energy through the sequence *chi*, while countering it with the earthy grounding of the *d*. The *l* adds a lilt of calmness, and the *s* a little unexpected excitement. So Childs really was the most fortuitous name I could think of. Although the whole lot is a bit of a mouthful, the shortened version – Isabella Childs – has a certain ring, and at least I won't be falling off mountains or tripping down steps in the foreseeable future.

Most people call me Izzie, which I like a lot.

So when I think about all that, I suppose that my name carries the aspirations of my mother, a kind of imperative to have a somewhat more educated and elegant life than her own; an ability to be fair minded; a divine ability to see both sides of every situation: a ghostly insistence that my ancestry, noble or otherwise be forever anchored within: and an ability to make my own identity in this world. *Izzie Childs*, the snaky seduction of the z's reverberating like a wolf in sheep's clothing, and the innocence of Childs married with the authority of my very own chosen surname.

Wow! More to that exercise than met the eye. Must make sure that Fenella reads this.

I can't believe that it's April and I'm in the Algarve. Brilliant surprise. I'm fifty this month, and have a sabbatical from college for a whole semester. I knew Henry was plotting something, but this has blown me away. I'm so lucky.

So, why is it that I sometimes feel that if I don't talk to someone, to just ramble and take stock of the last half century, I shall go absolutely stark staring mad? And when I say that, I imagine myself shouting and ranting and jumping and waving my hands around, feeling my eyes wide and wild, my hair standing on end, refusing to lie down no matter how much it is gelled or tweaked, and it's a strangely appealing image full of energy and liberation.

You know, I might just challenge Fenella a bit as to whether these mental exercises really are good for me. I am feeling very hot. Maybe I'm due my Naturwoman tablet (essential vitamins and minerals for the premenopausal stage of womanhood, or, in other words, most of your fertile life), and then perhaps a long relaxing swim.

I notice that there's a float by the poolside. Good. I can do some lengths using my legs only, which is fab for firming the buttocks.

Deep breaths now, Izzie, deep breaths.

about Henry

april 3rd 2010

'For the love of God! What a bloody liberty!'

Those were Henry's first words this morning, and it's not like him to be issuing expletives. I wondered what had happened overnight, given the very relaxed mood he seemed to be in when we went to bed.

We had a mellow day yesterday. Henry rescued me from the thirtieth frenzied length that the float and I had done using legs only, squatting at the side of the pool and offering me his arms to pull me up.

'D'you think I've done enough?' I found myself pathetically asking, 'I mean I want to look good for my birthday.'

'Izzie, you are a twit. You're perfectly f-f-fine. Really, stop f-fussing.'

He kissed me on the cheek.

'Come on, let's go mooching.'

I'd felt really grateful, saved from my demons, and pleased that Henry was feeling perkier.

'Just a little way, stay within ten kilometres or so, hey?'

So we drove up the coast a little and had our lunch at a beach café, *The New Wave*. We even splashed in the sea, and jumped the waves before relaxing in the sunshine. It was very calming, just what I needed.

And we'd not drunk much, what with the driving, just came back and sunbathed, read novels, and went to bed quite early, after a nightcap on the bedroom verandah. I felt refreshed at first light today, and assumed that Henry would too.

So I was surprised to hear him yelling when I emerged from the shower.

I ran into the bedroom.

'Henry, what's up?'

'This – this is what's up!' Henry was red in the face, and thrust his Blackberry at me. 'This!'

I patted in the remnants of Beauty Flash Balm which I'd just put on my cheeks, put down the Clarins body sculpting cream that was in my hand ready for action, and peered into the Blackberry.

There on the screen glared a memo from work. From Henry's father, James Chamberlain.

Henry has just been made a Managing Director. His job is to secure corporate training contracts on a global basis. To say that he treats his work as a labour of love is an understatement.

It's like he's always trying to make up for something, to his dad, really, and to some extent his mum, Mildred. His promise as Oxbridge material at school was scuppered when his first girlfriend snogged him a bad bout of glandular fever just before his 'A' levels. So he got poor grades and only accepted by his fifth choice of University. Reading, as it happens.

Which sounds fine to me, and, on the bright side, taught Henry both that sexual encounters carry a risk, *and* that it's okay to mix with the plebs. But it disappointed his parents, stuck up snobs that they are.

Henry then worked in personnel for a telecommunications company, and studied for his Diploma in Human Resources through the Open University. Then he got made redundant, though he did get a decent financial settlement.

I suppose if you work in personnel, you would approve yourself the best deal you could, wouldn't you.

Then Henry went to work for James. James is a bigwig in the corporate world. He drives a red Lamborghini, the word *compensating* reverberating in all our ears, him never knowing that the size of your *car* doesn't matter, actually. Henry's brief is to develop the 'new business' side of the training network.

It's been a struggle. In recession, training is the first thing out the window. *And* he's really worked to tame his stutter. It makes me so mad when people laugh at speech impediments. It takes some guts to stand up and speak out when you sound that little bit different.

Anyway, even though he's an MD, Henry continues to imagine that he disappoints his father. *I* think he's brilliant to work so effectively with James, who is not the easiest of men, let alone the easiest of fathers. *Total twat* would be another way to describe James, but Henry prefers me not to put it that way: he's a sensitive sort of soul. He's also very patient, and it takes a lot to disturb his equilibrium.

But the memo clearly had. I sat down on the bed and read it through.

James Chamberlain CEO [jameschamberlain@Go4It.com)
Sent: 3rd May 2010
To: Henry Chamberlain, Moira Whittaker, Paul Plumley,
Associates A-Z

It has come to my notice that certain individuals have not been acting in accord with the contract. Two things in particular have been highly unsatisfactory.

One, using telephones and facsimile machines at training venues. These are very expensive indeed and the bills are mounting up, so in future, please use your own mobile phone to contact HQ.

Two, one associate has recently been let go from the network after soliciting for work in his own name rather than that of the company. May I remind you *all* that such behaviour will not be tolerated and contracts will be terminated immediately if any associate or employee is found to be behaving in this unprofessional way.

Regards,

James Chamberlain. Chief Executive.

> I looked up at Henry.
> 'Typical James.'
> Henry nodded, and began to pace listlessly around the bedroom, waving his arms.
> 'I know, and w-what really gets me is that he can even *think* that this should be sent to me! I mean, as if I would.' He paused, looked out of the window, and then turned around to me.
> 'And, I should have been asked to deal with this. It's the training section.' Henry was shouting now, not stuttering any more. Never does when he's angry.
> I went to put my arms around him, but he shrugged me off. Then he telephoned HQ and was apparently reassured on several points, but clearly it was going to take a while for him to recover from his father's mistrust. I could see that his blood pressure, the instant barometer of his emotional life, was rising, his face red and his carotid artery visibly pulsating.
> 'Henry.'

I made him sit on the bed, and grounded myself before massaging his scalp in what I imagined to be the style of an Indian Head Massage.

'I'm alright.'

He moved my hands away, dismissing my attempts at TLC. I left him for a few moments and finished getting myself ready for the day. I remember Fenella teaching me that when a mood is hard to shift, try changing physiology, so when he came downstairs, I coaxed Henry into the pool and swam with him, hoping that the lull of the water might shift his emotional imbalance. And then I listened to him empathically for hours.

And hours.

To be honest with you, his bad energy was really starting to get me down. So then I decided to try changing environment, so we went out for lunch to Luz, which is just up the road. We found a South African restaurant, of all things. The drive was pretty, and Luz is spectacular, layers of red sandy rock cradling the bay which really is light, just like its Portuguese name: *luz*, after all, means light.

The restaurant was a real treat. We had ostrich schnitzel, fantastic, admired the view, chatted intermittently, but just as I thought Henry was really letting all that stupid work stuff go, things went wrong again when the waiter brought the bill.

'Th-thank you.' Henry smiled, and reached into his combat trousers for his wallet.

Which wasn't there.

I could see him checking every pocket, patting his legs and backside as if it might have been mysteriously sewn into a lining in error. He was puce.

'I'm so s-sorry,' he said, 'I really did think…'

'It's okay, sir.' The waiter, a dark South African man with a well cut shirt and equally well cut teeth, who I took to be the proprietor, was very calm.

'I can see that you have made a genuine mistake. Why don't you bring in the money when you are next passing?'

Henry hooed and hahed, coughed and spluttered, so I intervened.

'Thank you so much. We'll come back later today or tomorrow.' I loved the trust being offered here, didn't want it to be spoiled by Henry having a hissy fit, and knew there was nothing else to do.

26

Washing up was simply not an option. I mean, there's equality, and there's equality.

So then we drove back to the villa, where Henry found his wallet tucked into his Italian leather man bag which he treated himself to on a contract in Sorrento. He got changed, and went off for a late nine of golf, planning to pay the restaurant on the way back.

I was relieved when he left. It was mid-afternoon, and bloody great to get a little time to myself again without Henry's needs sapping my energy. I'd planned a self-hypnosis session today, to channel said energy into the rejuvenation of my face and neck. I've got a CD where you have to imagine the cells plumping and firming amid copious production of the super hormone, RDH. Really relaxing, and seems to work, as well.

Instead of that, though, once Henry was out, I walked down to the village. The air was fragrant with the smell of wild garlic which grows in abundance at the road side. The old men were once again sitting at the bus stop, obviously this was their regular meeting place. I bought some bread rolls from the *padaria*, the bakery, where I was served by a delightful woman with twinkly black eyes. *Boleenyas*, I thought she kept on saying, which I took to be the name for bread rolls – I'll have to look it up in my phrasebook. I thanked her and carried off the lovely fresh rolls in their paper bag.

Next I stopped in the newsagents just to get a couple of treats. There was a really nice man serving, and a woman I took to be his mother standing just behind him. I picked up a packet of Maltesers (the chocolates with the less fattening centre) and some cigarettes. Just in case. I had to ask for the cigarettes, as they were kept behind the counter.

'Menthol cigarettes?' I spoke slowly, enunciating carefully.

'*Cigarros?*' The man gestured at the range. I looked for familiar brands, couldn't see them.

'Menthol?' I saw a green and white packet and pointed; worth a go.

'Ah – ment-hal.' The man beamed and fetched a packet. I looked at them and nodded.

'Holidays?' he asked me, as I gave him a ten euro note and he looked for change.

'Yes, I'm here for a month,' I said. 'Just up the road.'

'First time in the Algarve?'

'Yes.'

'Very nice.' He gave me my change, smiled at me. 'My name is João. Enjoy yourself.'

'Thank you.' I put the change away, smiled at João, and the woman I took to be his mother came to the door with me and shook my hand.

You don't often get that in Birmingham.

I headed for the villa. On the way back, I noticed a group of men sitting outside a local café which sports a big tatty sign saying *Ricardo's*. They were English. I couldn't help overhearing the conversation.

'Yeah, I've got a place here, up the back of the Monte Alto, on the hill.' This utterance was delivered by a really fat guy with a broad Southern accent.

'Wassit like then, movin' over and everyfing like that?' A skinny younger guy drew hard on a Marlboro cigarette, and took a long swig of his beer.

'Well, not so bad.' The first guy also took a swill. 'Bloody difficult getting the Portuguese to do any work on time, mind, so you 'ave to 'ave the patience of a bloody saint. Alright, Ricardo?'

He nodded at the middle-aged Portuguese man who had materialized and was now taking empties from the table and changing the ashtray. Ricardo behaved as if he couldn't hear their arrogance as he served his English customers their fresh beers, while they spoke on as if he wasn't really there.

A kind of mutual sensory deprivation pact.

I ambled back to the villa, letting the sun bathe my shoulders beneath my straw hat, and once here I spread one of the fresh white rolls with sardine pâté, and ate it on the terrace, looking out over my lovely fields. Then I changed and lay down to read on my sunlounger. When I felt my afternoon snack was digested, I had a swim, poured myself a drink, and chilled, wedging myself comfortably into the very large blow up chair which some previous holiday makers have left. The chair is superb, has a well for a glass and an inbuilt tray for a book. So there I revelled, with my Pimms and lemonade and my book, *The Help*.

Bliss.

I was just dozing off when there came a knock on the big garden gate, and the two pool men that we'd seen on the first day let themselves through to the patio. I'd taken little notice of them when I'd seen them out of the window. I assumed that the dark one was Portuguese, though he didn't really speak, and the other English, probably about twenty-five.

Today I became aware while I was floating around that the English guy was good-looking and very friendly, smiling, commenting on the weather. I wasn't really sure what to do: my position wasn't the most seemly, and I was concerned that when they began the vacuuming process, they might inadvertently suck the edge of the rubber chair, and whip me round in a kind of whirlpool effect, or that I might drop my Pimms into the water.

Anyway, I said hello and after a decent interval, in which they assured me that it was fine to stay in the pool, and smiled a lot between themselves, I paddled myself to the steps and got out, just to be on the safe side. As I passed the young English man, he pushed his sunglasses up to his head, held out his hand to shake mine, and said, in a beautiful deep voice,

'My name's Joe, by the way, and I'll be looking after you from now on.'

I swear that as he said that he managed to look me up and down without moving his eyes (which are a very deep hazel colour and really sparkly), and I thought that perhaps he was flirting with me. Suffice to say that I did *not* push my Gucci sunglasses on to my head; rather, I appreciated the little mystery that they afforded me and the cover they provided my slight but inevitable wrinkles. A frisson flitted through my body, and I nearly giggled.

'I'll look forward to that, then,' I found myself saying. 'My name's Izzie.'

I relaxed carefully on to the sunbed while they worked, arranging my body to maximum advantage (stomach as flat as possible, legs bent to perfect angle, thighs slightly tensed) and I registered that Joe has a very good musculature. He's about 6' 2", bronzed, of course, and I revelled in watching the ripple of young flesh from a good vantage point.

I felt hornier than I had for ages, is the truth of it.

When they'd finished, I offered them both a drink, but Joe laughed, and said that they never drank on duty. He said 'perhaps another time', and they left.

Well, that seemed to me like a bit of a come-on, because I would only see him on duty, so when could another time be? And was he like this as a matter of patter, or had he genuinely found me attractive? Whatever the truth of it I noticed that when I plunged in to do my second bout of fifty lengths, I did so with renewed vigour.

When Henry came home, I surprised him by seducing him on the balcony as he got out of his golfing trews. Although he's not objectively as beautiful as Joe, at ten years my junior he's still pretty able, and gave me a bloody good seeing to.

It wasn't Henry's fault that he was unable to fully satisfy me, and he certainly never needs to know that that was left to me while he showered, and that it was Joe, not he, in my mind: thank God for keeping some privacy in even the closest of relationships. So everybody was happy and we went out again and enjoyed a good steak down in the village, several glasses of red wine, and now Henry has embarked on what I am sure will be a really good night's sleep, and it won't be long before I join him.

the non-immaculate conception of Constantine

april 4th 2010

I was outside on the patio this morning, having done forty lengths of the pool already, and now drinking fresh orange juice and eating one of those lovely buns from yesterday's trip to the *padaria*, when Henry came out.

'You've got mail.' He smiled at himself and dropped a piece of paper on to my lap. He'd gone to all the bother of printing out from the Blackberry on the lightweight printer that he takes in his business kit, just in case.

I raised an eyebrow.

'Thank you, Henry.' I was curious.

Then I saw that it was from Constantine, my first born. My heart rate raised the slightest bit as I picked up the paper to read.

From: Constantine161@gmail.com
To: ChildsandChamberlain@btinternet.com
RE: Birthday Visit

Dear Mother,

I hope that you are having a wonderful and relaxing time, and not drinking too much! All is well here, I have managed to secure five days off work now so will fly over on the 20th, arriving in Faro at 10.30 on the BA flight. Can you meet me from the airport or will I need to arrange a car?

Michael is working as hard as usual, and the children are fine. Pru has now started ballet lessons and loves them. Seb remains his active self; well actually he is a little hyperactive so I have banned all foods with an e number on them to see if we can calm him down a little. The child psychologist says there is nothing wrong with him that a little more careful discipline and regular bedtimes won't cure. Easy for him to say, he doesn't have to look after him! Anyway, Michael thinks it better for the children not to be taken out of school except in school holidays, so I shall be coming over on my own. I have never left them for so long before and hope that Polona, our fabulous nanny, will be able to cope. I must say that I am both excited and a little apprehensive, but of course wouldn't dream of missing your 50th, so my absence from home will have to be taken as a fait accompli.

Must dash, mother, as the floor waxers are coming soon, we have an important dinner party tomorrow night and Michael is keen that we show off the house to best advantage. Will look forward to seeing you.

Much love, as ever, Constantine.

I read the e-mail twice. What on earth was she on about?

'Henry, Connie seems to be talking about coming over.' I raised an eyebrow; saw that he was blushing slightly.

'Ah. Yes. Well.'

He handed me a fruit juice. He'd clearly prepared this while I read the e-mail.

'Well, actually, Izzie, I've arranged a bit of a do.'

I sucked through my straw.

'A bit of a do?'

'With the family. You and all the kids.' He slurped a little. 'A-a-and your mum.'

I nearly choked.

Oh Christ. We're having Abigail's party.

'What about *your* mum and dad?'

I was praying now, but to no avail. Henry was nodding, looking fearful, almost tearful.

'I couldn't l-leave them out.'

I agreed of course, could see the impossibility of that course of action.

'Jutta and Tammi are coming.'

Henry was holding onto my hand, smiling now, pleading with his eyes.

So I laughed.

What the hell. Jutta and Tammi, my two best friends, now we were cooking with gas. And it was a nice thought. No one's ever organized a party for me before, and it turns out that this is Henry's icing on my cake.

The month won't be dull, at any rate.

He still looked worried.

I kissed the top of his hand.

'Henry, you're a darling.'

While Henry took away our glasses, I reread the e-mail from my daughter, with the usual mixed emotions that Constantine – Connie – evokes.

I mean, who the fuck has floor waxers in? Connie's communication is typically polite and I would expect nothing less – she does everything properly. Including admonishing me, making sure that I am in check, my teetotal domestic daughter, alien spawn of my loins. I felt irritated at her, for that and for not allowing the little ones to take time off to come to my fiftieth birthday party. Yet I also think of her as 'poor Connie', and feel sorry for her, her life always seeming to be in tidy boxes (waxed, I shouldn't wonder). She's not unlike Attila. Not surprising I suppose, as Attila virtually brought Connie up.

For which I know I should be, and indeed am, eternally grateful. Connie was far from planned. I conceived her when I was just eighteen. I'd left home for University. I remember it well, Attila putting me on the train at Birmingham Snow Hill station for the long trip to Southampton, where I was to read English Literature. We'd worked towards this moment for ever, she and I, she working all the hours God could send, me studying my way through my scholarship at one of the best girls' schools in England. My 'A' level results weren't quite as perfect as they could have been, but they were good enough, and with an A for English, I got my University place.

My departure for Southampton was symbolic of so much for us both. Attila thoughtfully packed tissues alongside a lunch comprising Shipham's fish paste sandwiches, crisps, an apple, and a Kit Kat. She stood on the station platform, despite my exhortations that she leave before the train did. I told her that I wanted to spare her the indignity of possibly breaking down in public, but actually I wanted to spare myself the indignity of being associated with a woman who chose to wear a plaid check poncho with matching beret because she thought it was trendy. She insisted on 'being there for me', white hanky in hand, just in case I was overwhelmed with sadness as I ventured forth from home.

It was the opposite. I had to sit on my euphoria so that I could at least show a little consideration as she waved enthusiastically at me, making 'chin up' signs. I blew her a kiss as the train chugged me away, and it was only after we left the station, speeding past the desolate canals in Gas Street basin through the outskirts of the urban jungle of my childhood, that I felt my shoulders relax. I was thrilled: I was leaving home.

When I arrived at Southampton, wearing my homemade Laura Ashley smock top (why spend unnecessary hard earned cash on fancy clothes when we were perfectly adept with a Singer sewing machine?) and flared blue jeans, I was met by some older students and put on a bus to Hillfield Hall where I was to share a room, roommate yet unknown. I was one of the youngest freshers, and had to go to Hillfield as it was the only 'women only' hall of residence complete with full time warden. To my horror, I saw that it was surrounded by a tall wall topped with barbed wire and huge shards of broken glass. I wasn't sure whether this was to keep intruders (men, I presumed) out, or to keep us inmates from escaping.

Whatever their purpose, the vicious armaments proved themselves a comfort to my roommate who turned out to be manic depressive. On low days, she played Leonard Cohen on repeat on her Dansette record player, particularly *Suzanne*, cranking up her depression. Then she fantasised about how she could kill herself by throwing herself out of the window, wearing her long black velvet cloak, and impaling herself on to the jagged bastions of the wall below. She couldn't believe her luck at finding a potential suicide route so close to home.

Her name was Mona, and we turned out to get on surprisingly well, indulging each other's new found freedom to the hilt. Alcohol seemed a great way to shore up our confidence, and the Union bar was cheap. We found over the term that we could manage our finances quite well by living on a daily Mars bar and a steak and onion pie from the pub across the road. We then had plenty of money for Carlsberg Special Brew and Barley Wines. Occasionally we would cook in the shared kitchen, which was frequented by the God squad, probably the most possessive and uncharitable group of peasants you could ever wish to meet. The fridge was full of eggs with names on, Maria, Frances, Susan. I assumed that the egg owners hadn't gone as far as naming the embryonic chickens within, but were rather telling the rest of us to keep our bloody hands off. Clearly, we were far from the spirit of loaves and fishes (though some did draw that little fish symbol on the eggs, just to confirm that God was on their side in matters of ownership, I suppose).

That first week was a continuous party, events on every day and night. We were easily flattered by the attentions of the third year guys, clearly practised at spotting us nubile young freshers.

The night of the Freshers Ball was the climax to the week. The band was a bit of a B-lister by then, Mott the Hoople, but when they played *All the Young Dudes*, I felt like I'd arrived, because that described us so well – here I was, a young dude. After dancing all night, I felt really chuffed to have the attentions of Jeremy White, 'Jem'. He was a strikingly gorgeous third year Chemistry student, tall, with white blond hair and piercing blue eyes. We drank and danced all night, and I really felt I'd scored when Jem asked me to go home with him.

He helped me into a little blue Mini, and drunkenly drove me back to his place. I thought this fabulously trendy, down in the red-light area where the student houses were located. We went to his room, fell onto the bed, and began a bout of passionate sex. He unzipped his trousers and pushed my head down towards his penis which enthusiastically beamed up at me as if to say 'here you are, honey, I can't suck myself, you know.' I'd never had oral sex before: I was game for anything, tipsy and still dancing to the music in my head, stupidly feeling kind of honoured that Jem was offering me the privilege of satisfying his lust.

So I really was sorry when I became overenthusiastic, or perhaps it was that last barley wine, anyway I thought I'd blown it (so to speak) when I nibbled that little bit too hard and drew blood from his twitching member. All credit to Jem that after the first shout, and once he'd prized my jaws from the top of the aforementioned member, he recovered quickly, and devised a new pleasure strategy which he clearly considered safer.

More fool him.

'Here, get this under you.' He took out a large towel from his drawer, and tried to put it under my hips.

'Are we having a wash?'

I giggled at him but he kissed my mouth shut and then proceeded to sit up and put on a condom, which I tried to help with. I had no experience of this either, and my fumbling movements weren't exactly conducive to the heights of sexual passion. It didn't help that the condom was green and glowed in the dark. I think I might even have guffawed at the absurdity of it all. I mean, who *makes* these things?

Jem's ardour was made of firmer resolve than mine. He slipped on the device quite expertly, his fluorescent penis standing to full attention despite everything, and he proceeded to enter into the full spirit of it all, so to speak, while I smothered my laughter and made appropriate noises. There I was, losing my virginity. I seemed to be more spectator than participant, but I couldn't possibly stop as I believed that to do so would have been unfair. Something to do with feeling I'd led him on, or wondering what he'd do with all that excitement if he had to stop, as if he might explode or something.

So I closed my eyes and moaned and gyrated as fervently as I could. It wasn't long, certainly not more than a minute or two, before Jem shuddered, and I opened my eyes just at the point where his eyes rolled up into his head, leaving only the whites visible. I found this mildly disconcerting but reckoned that he must have achieved his orgasm, and for the first of many times in my life, I faked mine as best I knew how, which seemed to satisfy his expectations. We collapsed in a sweaty heap for a moment while our heart rates slowed down.

The deed being done, he withdrew his wilting member. The spectacle of his flaccid penis in its neon slimy shroud permeated my fuzzy brain, and I was tempted to laugh again. I imagined now that Jem would do the necessary and then return to hold or kiss me, perhaps to even thank me for my cherry, while we made plans into the future about how our relationship would go.

Instead, he made a strange gurgling noise in his throat.

'Oh my God,' he shrieked, 'fucking thing.'

'What?' I was bewildered.

'Look!' He pointed to my nubile thighs, and as I gazed at them, I realized that they were wetter than they should have been. The penny dropped. Not only had Jem exploded, as predicted, but so had the condom.

'Quick, don't move,' he yelled, and rushed over to the kitchen which was adjacent to the bedroom. I must have been much more sober by now, for I remember thinking that these were mixed imperatives and grammatically incompatible. Anyway, I did what I was told and could hear Jem muttering. He came to the doorway and yelled 'Is sperm alkaline or acid?' By now I was registering the kind of details that I'd rather not have, like how unprepossessing he looked in his shirt tails and socks. No man should ever be caught in this state, especially in or post *flagrante delecto*, a belief I carry with me to this day.

Jem disappeared back into the kitchen, and within minutes returned with a bottle of vinegar, a tin of Andrews liver salts and a wad of greaseproof paper.

'Lie down and keep your legs up,' he instructed. I complied without question. He proceeded to make a little funnel out of the greaseproof paper and inserted it into my vagina, and poured down the vinegar, which was cold and unpleasant, and told me to tighten my muscles and hold it in there for five minutes.

So, was this typically post-coital activity, then? I'd never seen it mentioned in *Cosmo*.

By this time I felt seriously lacking in dignity and insisted on an explanation. Jem looked at me intently, and must have registered the uncertainty in my eyes, for he suddenly metamorphosed from a manic chemistry student into a charming young man again, and sat beside me, taking my hand in his.

'Look,' he said, 'the condom burst and I'm trying to neutralise the sperm so that you don't get pregnant. But I can't remember now whether they're acid or alkaline, and I'm fresh out of litmus paper, so we need to douche you with vinegar and bicarbonate of soda, so that we cover all possibilities. It won't take long.'

'Aha.'

It all made sense now. This is only what you did if your condom burst. I nodded, and allowed him to follow the vinegar with a solution of the Andrews liver salts, apparently the closest thing to bicarb that he had in the kitchen. It was exceptionally fizzy to begin with, but thank God I had a firm pelvic floor in those days. I got the giggles again at one point, and Jem shouted as froth spurted out in projectile fashion all over his vigilant face. Then I waited till Jem reckoned it had been long enough, and welcomed the opportunity to go to the bathroom, sort myself out and get dressed. Jem ushered me out fairly quickly into his Mini and drove me at speed to Hillfield Hall.

I knew not to ask if I'd be seeing him again.

I staggered in past the night porter, went to my room and grabbed a towel. Mona muttered something, but I was already leaving again on my way to the communal bathroom.

It was a relief to fall into the bath, even though by then it was 4 a.m. and I was risking the wrath of the Christians with the noise of the running water, but to be honest, I didn't care. I just soaked until I tired myself out and then went back to my room. I fell into my bed across from Mona. She hadn't pulled that night and was lying on her bed listening to *Suzanne*, I could see how this really could take us down, and for a second I could fully understand the pull to self-impalation. Happily, I chose instead to turn over and sleep.

I didn't see much of Jem after that, just now and then in the coffee bar or in the Union. The memory of the bicarb and vinegar, illustrated in my mind with a green neon penis, was not one I wanted to revisit any more than necessary.

It was another four months before I realised that neither douche had worked, and that I was pregnant with the budding foetus who was to become Constantine. It was another month after that before I had the courage to tell Attila. I knew that I couldn't have an abortion, not at that stage. I celebrated the end of my first year away by becoming a mother myself for three whole months before I agreed that I would leave Constantine with her Nana and resume life as a student as if nothing had happened. After all the work we had put into getting me to University, it was settled that the degree must go on.

And anyway, Attila was missing a life project and was only too pleased to begin again the cycle of providing for someone who would have life easier than she.

As I left Birmingham station for a second year, I welcomed the tissues in my leaving pack and cried all the way to Winchester, the tears that I had been too scared to let go at home now waterfalling down my cheeks. Blotchy-faced and flat-stomached again, I arrived at Southampton on a Thursday, blocked my responsibilities out of my mind and vowed to go for a first-class result. By Friday morning I was collecting my contraceptive pills as I prepared for another year of excess, only this time working into the early hours every other week night so that I wouldn't let Attila down in return for her huge sacrifice. A guilty bargain with myself.

Later on, I did take Constantine to live with me, yet our relationship has always been a strange one because I think she sometimes feels that I let her down. And I think, really, that I did.

I know that Fenella always says that all we have is the now and the future, yet sometimes my past is like a stone in my shoe, it just niggles away. I would so like to break free from the chains of guilt that I associate with Connie.

    What do you want instead of guilt? I hear Fenella ask.

    And you know what, I just want to be relaxed with Connie, real, honest, and spontaneous.

    I dictated a reply for Henry to tap out onto the Blackberry.

'Constantine, how lovely to hear from you. I was sorry at first that the kids aren't coming, your husband is just ludicrous at times. But now I think about it, I'm kind of glad you will be here alone so we can catch up together, and have a drop of champagne or two. Will pick you up from the airport. Looking forward to it. Love, Mum. Xxx'

'Thank you,' I said, as Henry sent my message through the ether, 'thank you.'

golfing

Well, here I am with a large gin and tonic (clean out of Pimms), and a nifty cigarette, which feels so-o-o good. I know that Henry's right when he says it's a disgusting habit: but there are times when breathing deeply or sucking on a liquorice bark just won't do. This is one of them. I'm on the verandah upstairs, can you imagine, hiding like a naughty schoolgirl. But you know, I love the illicitness of that, and really needed to get away from the guests we've acquired downstairs. I will of course re-emerge on the terrace shortly and fulfil my hostly obligations. For now it's bloody marvellous to be on my own, and I'm just recording this onto my iPod, *sotto voce*, before we go out, to get it off my chest, so it's ready to upload.

We've just played a game of golf on what must be the hardest course in the Algarve (if not the bloody world, I wouldn't wonder) with some business acquaintances of Henry's, Fred and Antonia Blackley. Fred and Antonia are very influential at the golf club, *Parque da Montanha*, and Henry, bless, has taken the opportunity to try to woo them for new business. He's a little twitchy at having this month off, and is desperately trying to please that old goat James. He knew that the Blackleys were going to be here, so decided to court them as some kind of atonement (for what, I don't know – don't even go there – that bloody family).

Golf is not my strong suit. Frankly, I never thought I'd be one of those snobs rushing round a golf course brandishing a stick, trying to get a bloody stupid ball into a bloody stupid hole, but there you have it. Apparently, it's all the rage these days, and I understand that many heroes of my youth, like Alice Cooper and Lou Reed, now love to play golf: whether that makes it more or less sad is anybody's guess. Henry insisted that I learn, and bought me a set of clubs, Ping, or Pong, or something, and treated me to twenty lessons with a golfing pro, who I found sweaty and distasteful, not at all like that young pool man – now if *he'd* been teaching me it might have been different – but he's not relevant to my story, so I don't know why I'm even thinking about him.

Anyway, Henry has this theory that 'they who play together stay together', and therefore I can play golf, badly, erratically, with some little pleasure. What I can't stand, and draw the line at, is Club House obsession, and the post-match deconstruction of every game, nay every hole, every stroke, holds about as much interest for me as a wet kipper. I think it self-indulgent, and if I'm going to be self-indulgent, there are more pleasurable and private ways I can think of to be so.

I digress. Fred and Antonia had to be wooed, and I was quite happy to help Henry to do that – or so I thought. Well, in the event, what a carry-on. Henry and Fred drove the buggies, and I was left to accompany Antonia, thirty-something and size 10, as she whined and whinged her way round the course. She kept on talking dribble, such things as 'it must be *marvellous* to be that little bit older, Fred tells me that you'll soon be fifty, how frightfully freeing', and, 'the trouble with being a small size ten is that it's awfully difficult to find golf clothes to fit', so that I had to bite my lip before I said something trite and very rude, like 'oh fuck off, you stupid little tart', as I checked for the whisker under my chin: and I had that image again, me with the arms waving and shouting and feeling great, and I had to put all my energy into the game (which I must say worked well on the seventh when I hit a cracking drive, straight onto the green, and parred the hole).

Antonia had no such luck. Fred had to choose her clubs for her at more or less every swing, and when he was too far ahead with the buggy, she used this kind of walkie-talkie device to ask his advice, a habit that really began to annoy me. And then, I swear, after three bad holes on the trot, she began to cheat. She counted all her strokes retrospectively, rather than when she played them, and invariably lost one or even two in the process so that her scores, which in reality were worse than mine, always beat me. I was put out. Once is a mistake, but this was clearly a deliberate strategy. So each hole that I played really well was negated by Antonia Moanier knocking strokes off left right and centre. It was very awkward, and highly demotivating.

What was I to do?

And that's when I let myself down. In fact, I let me down, I let Fenella down, I let the whole sisterhood down.

The solution was obvious. By the thirteenth I began to cheat too. Nothing so mundane as counting, I might add, and actually, as I recall them, I'm really quite proud of my innovations. The thirteenth hole, you see, has an elevated tee and you have to hit the ball over a fairly long lake on to quite a small green which resides on the top of a hill, like the zenith on a pimple. Basically, this means that if your shot is not accurate enough, you find yourself at the bottom of said hill with your silly stick, trying to hit the ball upwards towards a ridiculously small hole that you can't even see.

Well, that was where I found myself after my drive, forlornly at the bottom of the hill. Antonia had already had two shots which everyone had noticed, and was now beyond the green, so little room for a cheat on that one, and Fred and Henry had both gone too far. So suddenly I realised that I was on my own at the bottom of this hill, tired, fed up, and with the motivation of a pig on its way to the abattoir. I don't know what possessed me, but I impulsively just picked up my golf ball and threw it, over arm, and watched with gratitude as it disappeared over the aforementioned hilltop onto what I supposed was the green.

Imagine my delight when I heard a great shout go up from the others, for the ball had made its way not only onto the green but also into the hole, and I'd scored a birdie!! In the hole in two! I ran up the hill, golf club waving about my head, and whooped it up with Henry who, bless, was so proud of his talented wife, and do you know, I never even blushed.

Well, Fred congratulated me with a big hug, and Antonia kissed the air near my cheek and said 'wow, a birdie, I wish I was old enough and experienced enough to get one of those', and so that was it, any hint of shame was obliterated and I entertained myself hugely by spending the rest of the game inventing good ways to cheat. I liked the one where my ball had completely disappeared into the rough and I dropped another down the inside of my trouser leg to an advantageous position, like James Bond in *Goldfinger*. Another time, when I had hit a long drive just to the edge of the fairway (that's the shaved bit down the middle) but was left with the ball just in slightly long grass, I niftily placed a tee peg underneath it before hitting it again, which makes the shot a lot easier, and I managed to par again! To make things even better, Antonia also made a long shot into the rough, and I came across it before her so I stood on it to make it plug right down into the ground before shouting, in my most helpful voice, 'it's here, Antonia, I think it's unplayable', so that she had to take a penalty shot.

Other than that, for those last few remaining holes, I played her at her own game – literally. I didn't add up until I was on the green, and then I'd say 'What did you score on that hole, Antonia', and when she purred her lying little answer, like 'five', I'd say, 'Oh, I must have got a four then. I know I was on the green in one less than you – funny, it felt like more', and there was nothing she could do.

Anyway, Antonia was mad, and pouted and sulked the rest of the way around. So I just had to get away for a few moments now that we're back in our lovely villa, and leave her to be common and vulgar out on the terrace. She is one of those women who always wants to know how much things cost, and likes to let you know how pricey her clothes were, or what good quality silk they are made of, and how she got them in a sale, a habit which I find most distasteful.

So there, there *are* habits which are worse than mine, and my lovely menthol cigarette is finished now. Not quite a two-facing Janus today, was I, more a two-faced woman of quite a different kind – and I tell you, it feels so, so good.

I'm going for a shower. Then we're going to a very posh restaurant, and Henry will fawn some more, and Antonia will bitch, and Fred, who I shall flirt with, will be nice. Then I shall muster the experience of my nearly great age to help Henry secure the business and I shall drink red wine, probably too much of it, until yet another day in paradise is over.

Stefan, Stig and stubbed toes

april 6th 2010

'Bastard.'

That was my greeting this morning. Henry, no less, swearing again. He threw his Blackberry onto the bed.

'Bastard.'

'James?'

I raised an eyebrow at my husband. He nodded. I picked up the Blackberry and read. As previously, a memo to all staff.

Following my last memo, it has come to my notice that certain individuals have still not been observing professional behaviour and boundaries. Not only have they taken liberties with the telephone facilities, but I gather that one trainer has had sexual liaisons with a delegate, the height of unprofessional behaviour.

I imagined that it was both common sense and ethically binding that you do not, DO NOT, have sex with the delegates. To make this absolutely clear to everyone, and to preclude any further slights on this organization, I shall be expecting each of you to attend a special workshop which will be facilitated by Henry, Moira and Paul within the next two months, on codes of conduct, and terms and conditions of association to this organization.

All associates are expected to attend. Details to follow,

James Chamberlain. Chief Executive.

And on Henry's copy, there, written at the end, was a simple instruction – *get on to it*.

I laughed.

'Well, it makes a change for him not to be doing the screwing, anyway – he'd sell his own aunty if it made him some money.'

It didn't go down well.

Henry can be a bit sensitive about sexual matters at the best of times, so off we went again, me making soothing noises and drawing Henry's attention to the beautiful surroundings, and trying to put things into perspective, before leaving him to his inevitable phone calls, and, somewhat unusually for him, to a large glass of red wine, even though it was before eleven.

I went out to get some sun, lolloping on the blow up chair and loving it. The phone went several times. I heard it vaguely from my reveries but ignored it, thinking, as Fenella has taught me, *locus of control, locus of control* – I couldn't control what was going on, so why spend energy on it. Why worry in the slightest, indeed? Instead, I thought about that young pool man, as today was the day I was expecting him and his friend to come.

I was surprised when Henry appeared red-faced on the terrace holding out the phone.

'It's Stef,' he grunted, handing it over to me, and wandered off, gulping down the last of his wine. I put the phone to my ear.

'Stef?'

Stefan is my youngest son, one of those young men for whom life is an easy cruise, each stop in each port leading seamlessly to the next.

'Hey, Mum, how you doing out there. Everything cool?'

'Stefan! Everything's great. How about you?'

'Chilled, Mum, chilled. How's that old beast Henry, he sounded a bit high?'

I envisioned Henry in my mind's eye, Hawaiian shirt open down his chest, face red and puffed up, empty wine glass in hand.

'Very Henry like, not quite so chilled as you, as you so rightly spotted, but getting there. You know how it is.'

'I do, I do. Now then, flights. I've got some good deals going and can fly via Stansted on the 18th. Can't wait to get the vibes of sunny Portugal. How's the local talent?'

A vision of Joe flitted before my eyes. I tried to imagine how Stefan would find the local talent in Portugal. I have never been entirely sure of his sexual preferences and imagine that he would have to try both genders simply because he can, so it is conceivable that he might fancy Joe. I might be wrong. I laughed.

'Well I don't see it through your eyes, son, so you'll have to judge for yourself. That's great about the flights, Stefan; I really look forward to seeing you.'

'There's two flights, Mum, I'm hoping to bring a friend, Chris. Is that okay?'

I took the executive decision.

'That's fine. Let me know what time you're arriving and I'll pick you up or arrange a taxi. E-mail the details to Henry, he'll like that.'

'I will.'

'How are the exams, Stef?'

'So far, so good, very easy, lots of stuff on Freud and Klein. I'll tell you about it when I'm there, maybe over a red wine.'

'Brill. I look forward to it. See you on 18th. Ciao.'

And that was it; a typical phone call with my lovely son. Stefan doesn't really do phones. He's reading Human Sciences at the University in Copenhagen, and is a lot like his dad, with all his best bits, and a touch of my nature at its most bohemian.

Some would say promiscuous, but that's not a word I like much.

Stefan's dad. I made my way to a sunbed, and found myself thinking back to when I met him, on a girly weekend with my dear friend Jutta.

We'd arranged the weekend because Jutta was feeling low, and said she'd needed a break with company. I was only too happy to be the company. I had three children by then, and was doing my best to make ends meet on a teacher's salary. I was just embarking on some tutoring for the Open University, and was also a life model for the local art college. I was tired. Once, when I was posing nude, I found myself falling into a bit of a sleepy haze, slipping off the stool on which I was positioned, right into someone's oil palette. A bit embarrassing really, though the artist was very understanding, and asked me just to sit on his canvas so that the colours became imprinted by my flesh – impressionism at its most literal.

Jutta is remotely Danish, her great grandmother providing those Nordic genes. The cut of Jutta's jaw and her strawberry blond hair would have gone well under a Viking helmet, certainly more so than under the woolly hat type creations that tended to grace the robust features of the Wakefield side of her family. Anyway, she wanted to get back to her roots, and I was glad to provide the companionship. I made the booking for us, farmed out my three children with various friends and family, and we arrived at the airport one unseasonably warm Thursday night in May, 1991.

We checked in and made our way to the airport lounge, initially for vodkas. We'd booked Business Class. It cost an arm and a leg, but Jutta paid as she'd had a bit of a windfall. Her aunt had died after tripping over a raised manhole cover while running to the Post Office to pick up her pension in time to get to the local bookies, and Jutta was her beneficiary. Hence Jutta's sense of depression coupled with her yen for the land of her ancestry.

We were delighted by the executive lounge, vodka paling into the land of dull as we were faced with a huge liquid buffet of Pimms, Malibu, Baileys, champagne, you name it, it was there. We were like children in a sweet shop. After the first drink, we heard that our plane was delayed, so we had another. At which point I happened to brush arms with a fairly hunky looking guy, blond hair, ice blue eyes, tanned face, great smile. We were both reaching for the champagne at the same time.

'Sorry,' I said, backing off.

'No problem. May I?'

He took the bottle, and poured for me and for Jutta.

'Would you mind if we joined you?' He inclined his head toward his companion. I nodded agreement.

'Please.'

So it was that we joined company, and got chatting. Turned out his name was Stig and he was a Professor of *Philosophy*, no less, from the existentialist school – 'to be or not to be', and all that. And of course the details: if one is to be, then there are questions of *who* to be and *what* to be, whether to be sober or tipsy, good or bad. Since I was in one of my reflective phases, Stig couldn't have shown up at a more opportune time. I was familiar with all of these deeper questions. A philosopher was precisely what I needed, to play Sartre to my de Beauvoir

Stig's friend Carsten was an experimental psychologist. This was right up Jutta's street, as she was in the midst of some of her deeper psychological training. She had been rebirthed just the week before, so they had loads to talk about.

'So what do you mean, a proper psychologist? I mean, what kind of people put pigeons in a glass box, chase rats through mazes, and try and get mice to walk planks, just to see how soon they learn not to fall in the water? You'll have to work hard to convince me of Skinner over Freud – come on, now, give it your best shot.' Thus spake Jutta as Carsten returned from the bar with yet another drink.

Amazing what passes for flirtation amongst psychologists.

Two hours later, our delayed flight became a cancellation due to engine trouble, and we were all dispatched, somewhat tipsily, to a nearby hotel. I felt giddy, in more ways than one. We arranged to have dinner together, and I just knew that Stig and I would end up in bed. He was seductive, his Danish tones making his predictability acceptable.

'You know, Izzie, you have the most beautiful eyes,' he said to me, somewhere between the oysters and the sole meunière. 'They make me want to drown in your essence.'

Okay, so it sounds corny now, but I can't tell you how that thrilled me at the time. At some point in the evening, I asked him outright if he wanted to sleep with me. He answered forcefully, in deep tones.

'Kandura said that the desire for shared sleep is a desire entrenched in love, love for one woman only. I would not presume that privilege with you yet.' He paused. 'But the desire to make love – that, dearest Izzie, is another question.'

Stig and I stayed awake all night, making love, drinking a little more, talking about the meaning of life. And by the morning, we decided that who knew or cared if love or life were futile, we might as well enjoy them both to the full, and went for breakfast on very good terms.

We did eventually get to Copenhagen, where Jutta and I had a wild time cruising round and exploring. Not many roots were discovered, but there you go.

In short, the truth of the matter was that for the want of a working engine, a babe was conceived. And when, some months later, I approached Stig on the subject of his baby being in a state of 'about to be', I have to say that he was a gent. He visited me twice before Stefan's birth, and several times after. We continued a sexual side to our relationship for two or three years, while developing a deep sense of friendship. He was and is devoted to Stefan, having him over weekends and school holidays. And now Stefan studies in his ancestral city. Gestalt.

Anyway, I was remembering all this, and had almost dropped off on the sunbed, when I heard a bit of a kerfuffle; some clattering noises, a horse neighing, and a shout, seemingly Henry, apparently coming from the road. Then another shout, *definitely* Henry.

48

'Whoa, steady on, steady on,' he was yelling. I got up and looked over the wall.

The young foal from the field over the way was trotting down the middle of the road, and Henry was trotting after him.

'Whoa, there now, whoa!' Henry was shouting with considerable gusto: he was brought up in rural surroundings, and is very familiar with animals, deeply comfortable. My chest swelled a little at his courage as he charged off to rescue the foal from danger.

My pride was well deserved. Henry, bless, managed to bring the foal – which is a good three months old, apparently, and quite large – up the road, but just as he was on the last leg of the rescue, there was a nasty snort, a stomp, and a yell. The foal had stamped on Henry's foot.

'Bugger!'

Still Henry persevered, tenaciously guiding the animal back into the field. A Portuguese man with a dark beret type hat came running down from behind the derelict farmhouse on the hill, and took the foal from Henry, who was by now redder than ever, and limping quite markedly.

'Obrigado,' the man, who we now know to be called Armindo, said to Henry, shaking his hand and nodding a lot. I was clapping enthusiastically from the sunbed on which I was now standing, hanging over the wall. I could see the shape of the man's mouth, and knew what he was saying – 'obrigado' was the word for thank you, I'd looked it up in my *Portuguese in a Month* phrase book that I'd found on the bookshelves in the villa. *Ob-ree-gard-oooh.*

Henry looked really chuffed, but then as he began to limp home, I saw to my horror that Armindo began to pelt the poor foal with rocks, shouting at it while leading it up the field. Henry turned back at the commotion, and initially moved toward the man, but then moved away again. We both generally agree that it's rarely wise to interfere in local customs. Armindo looked quite daunting, arms flailing and voice very loud, so Henry looked at me and shrugged and continued to limp back over to the villa. I whipped on my sarong and fit flops and went to meet him as he hobbled in through the gate, which is when I saw the extent of the damage to his foot.

Left big toe, to be exact.

Henry was sure that the toe was not broken, but there is a seriously nasty bruise (and it wouldn't surprise me still if he doesn't lose that toenail). At any rate, I insisted that we go to a doctor. The nearest surgery was not far away, so off we trogged and found our way following the directions from the guest manual.

The doctor was very thorough.

'You are tourists?'

His English was excellent.

'Yes,' Henry said, 'we are.'

'Hmm.' The Doctor wrote something down.

'When was last Tetanus?'

'Th-three years ago.' Henry grimaced. The toe was giving him some gyp now.

'Hmm. I think another one.' The Doctor displayed a white toothed grin, just a sparkle of gold visible in some far corner. 'And blood tests. Just in case.'

Henry opened his mouth to protest, but the Doctor raised a hand to shush him.

'And something for the pain, I think?' He raised an eyebrow, and Henry nodded. So Henry had two injections, one in the arm and one in the backside, and then went to the nurse to have blood taken for analysis on the premises.

While we were waiting for the results, we picked up a guide book on Lagos. Lagos is the nearest town, steeped in history, and a bit more than a fishing village. It goes back over two thousand years, full of Roman ruins, and has a more recent Moorish influence, which I know I'll just love.

'Henry,' I said, 'let's do a guided tour one day, look, there's all this culture.' Henry nodded, reluctantly. He's never been a great one for city explorations. 'And we should make it soon. We've been in Portugal for almost a whole week now, so it's about time you closed down the Blackberry and the Laptop. I want some real fun, toe or no toe.'

Henry looked at me intently.

'Well,' he said, 'I suppose I did spend a lot of time before we came insisting that you go with the surprise, and that it's important to face new challenges.'

I smiled.

'And actually, we've hardly done any of the holiday things we usually do, while I still have work on my mind. So sod it, Izzie, you're right. Stuff work.'

And he did no more than turn off his Blackberry there and then, and took charge of the guide book.

'Let's have a look what's there.'

I could see him turning quickly past the pages on castles and so on, until his eyes lit up when he came to the section on beach activities. He lingered over pictures of boats leaving the marina with eager young faces aboard, faces belonging to people who were going diving, or paragliding.

So by the time he was called back in to the doctor for the results of the detailed blood analysis, we were considering our beach options. Our bubble of excitement was only lightly pricked by the consultation bill, which was over 320 euros, as luckily we can get it back on insurance. We have to keep an eye on the swelling, and if it's not down in three days, they will arrange an x-ray. I couldn't quite get the doctor's name, I thought it was Dr Jorges something, but then I thought that I heard a couple outside say something that sounded like Dr Invoice. It'll be on the paperwork for the insurance, I guess.

I drove us there and back and was quite pleased with myself, quickly got used to the left hand drive. We stopped at a little café on the roadside and treated ourselves to a *bifana,* a kind of sliced pork sandwich, a local specialty, lovely and tender, oozing strong garlic. Then we stopped off at the local supermarket and bought some salad ingredients for our supper – feta cheese, avocado, ripe tomatoes, fresh lettuce, olives, the usual suspects. The man in the shop was round-faced and very friendly, suggesting all sorts of accompaniments so that in the end we bought some unknown vegetable as well, some red wine, and two bottles of *vinho verde,* the local green wine. The shop keeper smiled at us approvingly, as we picked up things to try, and put them in our basket. It was all quite pleasant really, getting to know the village a bit more, and it was only as we approached the villa and I saw a white truck turning out of our drive, its tail gate preceding me into the distance, that I realised we'd missed the pool men. I felt disappointed, then guilty, because after all, Henry was lucky to get off with a bruised toe. It could have been much worse, he might have been trampled to death. Then where would I be?

Single again, at my age.

Really.

So I counted my blessings. We both showered, and took a bit of a late nap. I did that happiness exercise, the one where you identify three things to be thankful for each day, Fenella told me about it. I've seen it on *Make the Midlands Happy*, a breakfast telly venture with happy tips on every day for a week. I decided to be happy about Henry's courage; Henry's safety; and then the fact that I am still alive enough of spirit to even think about the pool men.

Man.

We had our supper outside on the patio, and I lit candles, citronella to keep the mossies away. We ate pâté and cheese with the salad, and drank wine, *Terras d'el Re*i. Henry had chosen it because it came from the Alentejo region, one of the chief wine producing regions, apparently. The bottle sported a label showing a woman in a ragged dress picking grapes, giving the impression of energy and earthiness. It spoke to me like an invitation to grab hold of life and taste it to the full.

Though the wine itself was not, as it happens, that outstanding.

But it was medicinal, and by the end of the evening, when we were down to the last glass, and had further examined the guide book which he'd purloined, Henry decided that we should make our minds up about whether we would do culture vulture sightseeing, or adventurous activities. I ruled out culture vulture because I knew it doesn't appeal to him, and on the crest of my appreciation exercise, I felt that Henry should have some fun. As to what activity in particular we should go for, we decided on the toss of a euro.

Paragliding.

The sunset was beautiful. Dusk is swift here, night's inky cover replacing daylight in seamless transition. Then the sky is superb, a clear roof thronged with stars as bright as you can imagine, thousands of them twinkling at us like beady little eyes.

So it's been all go, and a funny kind of day, mixed emotions for me, and probably for Henry too. He's quite settled outside still, with a *maciera*, a kind of local brandy, a night cap, he said. He thought it would be good for the shock and the upset as well as the toe. He's reading one of the books he's brought with him, by the light of the stars and the candles and I've told him that I'll be down in a minute. The day might have been a little unpredictable, but the mood of the Algarvian night has worked its soothing magic, just as it did yesterday.

I love this place, it's getting under my skin. I can't wait to go out more. And neither can I wait for my friends to arrive.

A party. What a brilliant idea.

paragliding

april 7th 2010

What a day! What a fantastic day, one of the best of my life. I flew, I well and truly flew – and it's amazing!

I have to give Henry his due, once a decision is made he's not slow to act. So when today dawned, he examined his toe, which has calmed significantly, and pronounced himself fit to paraglide. We mused over coffee about what we should wear. Henry favoured tracksuits, on the basis that anything too tight, and the crotch might feel restricted. I favoured shorts, seeing this as an opportunity to get my legs even browner than they are already: but my shorts are wide legged and Henry was concerned that my knickers would show when seen from below. In the end, I went with his suggestion, but added a white Armani T-shirt to my outfit, and so we drove off to Lagos in our T-shirts and jogging bottoms, me with my sun cream and shades, Henry with the video camera.

'No videoing chins from underneath, now, remember?'

I have to remind him of these things.

Paragliding. I've watched people paraglide on various holidays, admiring the elegance of flight, gliding along like a bird. I knew it would be amazing. I was surprised, then, to find that I had butterflies in my stomach as we got nearer to Lagos. I confessed them to Henry, and he thoughtfully caressed my knee; so much so that I had to ask him to stop after a few minutes, as his circle of affection was becoming smaller and smaller. He was like an adolescent lover, you know, the kind who finds a spot which he believes to be erogenous and thinks that if he rubs it determinedly enough, you will be overwhelmed with waves of passion and release.

Instead of which you just become sore.

We drove down into the sweep of the Lagos bay, along the Avenida, the statue of Henry the Navigator on the right, proudly surveying his territory. It's not that long apparently since Lagos was where slaves were brought into Portugal from Africa, hence its name. Beyond the statue we could see across to the Marina. Where once the schooners sailed into port, delivering their frightened cargo, now there lay rows of yachts and pleasure cruisers.

On the left hand side of the road was the big market where the slaves were sold, fresh fish its reluctant captives these days. We drove past, following the signs to the Marina, and within five more minutes we were there and parked up. We walked through a small alleyway and the full majesty of the yacht infested waters and bijou shops and cafés greeted us. Dotted around the water's edge were kiosks for booking water sports.

'Wow.' I was excited.

'Which one do you think, sweetheart?' Henry perused the sights before him, sounding assertive. He was on a mission, and he was loving it.

I squeezed his hand.

'I'm not sure,' I said. 'I imagine they're much of a muchness.'

Henry nodded.

'We'll go red.'

He led me off to the nearest kiosk, pillar-box red, serviced by a fit looking Portuguese guy.

'What time is paragliding?' he said.

'Just half an hour, sir.' The kiosk owner smiled.

Henry looked at me, and I nodded, so he proceeded to book the trip.

I felt proud of him, then. He stuttered only once as he tried out his pigeon Portuguese. Both Henry and I believe that if you are going to go to someone's country, you should at least learn how to say 'please', 'thank you', 'yes' and 'no' in their language. Unfortunately, the Portuguese for 'please' is *se faz favor*, (sounds like 'fash favor'), and f is Henry's most difficult sound. It took him half a minute to finish his 'Dois paragliding, fa-fa-fa-fa-fash fa-fa-fa-vor, obrigado senhor'.

The dark-eyed, dark-haired kiosk owner looked at Henry curiously then said in perfect English,

'No. It's just *faz favor*. How many was it for again?'

Henry repeated his request, to be absolutely clear, and as a matter of principle, until the vendor's assistant and one or two people in the queue began to realise that he hadn't made a mistake with his words, but had a speech impediment. To their credit, they didn't try to humiliate him: they began instead to encourage him, so that when Henry finally got the words out, a small cheer went up and the vendor shook his hand.

'And for you, Senhor, a discount: we will make a longer trip for the same money.' Henry was chuffed, and his final *obrigado* was uttered clearly and fluently. We high-fived and Henry was flushed with pleasure as we walked off hand in hand.

We sat and had a non-alcoholic cocktail while we waited, and enjoyed the view, naming which yacht we'd fancy if we had the choice. Then we made our way over to our red stand, and watched our boat come in.

'They look a nice strong crew, anyway.' Henry gestured to the two sailors who moored the boat and helped the last passengers off.

And then we boarded.

Those butterflies were going again in my stomach, so once we were racing out seaward, I asked Henry if he would mind if I went first. I've learned over the years that the best way to confront fear is to face it as soon as possible. Henry, bless, acquiesced, and then my butterflies all beat their wings in unison, slowing down in harmony until they were totally at rest.

The two hunky sailors instructed us to put on life jackets, covering my Armani T-shirt after all. As we pulled out of the harbour, I felt at one with the world, the sun lighting up the sea with diamonds, and the feeling of freedom entering my very pores. I squeezed Henry's hand when I could get at it. He was videoing away, as we moved steadily along the coast of marbled rocks and sandstone cliffs. He was particularly entertained to spot a little inlet where naked men were bathing, and he zoomed in with glee. I made a mental note to let Stefan know about it, just in case.

Once we were far enough out to sea, the taller of the two sailors beckoned me across to the stern of the boat and helped me into the parachute harness. He explained that I would stand on the end of the boat and he would let out the rope gently, and I would just go up. My karma was excellent, until just before I was to be launched, when he spoke.

'And *senhora*, whatever you do, you must never gesticulate too much with your arms, or pull on the ropes with your hands, like this.' He waved his arms out to his sides, and pulled up and down. 'Or else the parachute will go out of control.'

Why do people do that? Make suggestions, I mean. Until that moment, I had no intention of pulling on the ropes at all, but I was now convinced that it would be impossible not to. I took a deep breath, while he added another complication.

'Unless,' he said, 'you look down and see me waving to the left or to the right, and then it is imperative that you must pull on the side to which I am referring.'

I was just about to ask more, when lo and behold, he grinned and began to loosen out the rope.

I eased up into the air and within a minute or two was so high up that I was surrounded by sky, by blue, and warmth, and profound peace.

I, Isabella Childs, was flying, and I loved it. I had felt the fear, and done it anyway! I don't really know what I was thinking, perhaps it was Nirvana and I had reached the Buddhist state of no thought. I was walking in the air, feeling free as a bird. Nothing existed except the Now☺.

I was so high up I could hardly see the people on the boat at all.

People on the boat.

My karma shifted: what if the sailor was trying to send me a signal? I looked down, waving to indicate my freedom, slightly anxious that I might rock myself. Barely a move. So I waved with the other arm, and then, when that seemed okay, I put both arms out together in defiance of my fears and still everything was fine. I guffawed and shouted with pleasure. I was the wild-haired woman of my fantasy, only without the anger, and it was great.

Then I looked down and noticed movement on the boat. I made myself focus in to see if they were motioning to me in case I needed to do anything. With concentration, I could see all three figures, and I was sure that one of them was waving his left arm out. I was just about to pull on the rope, when I noticed him wave the right arm. Then both together. I began to mirror the movement, pulling on each rope in turn until the parachute was lurching unsteadily from side to side. This couldn't be right. I noticed that I was losing height. While somewhat alarming, this also meant that I could see my sailors more clearly. Yes, they were both gesticulating now, and one was winching in the rope. I continued to pull left and right to the point of nearly doing a full somersault, and I was sure I heard one of them say 'stupid woman', which didn't exactly fill me with confidence. I tried desperately to reclaim the sensation of freedom which was beginning to slip through my fingers, and indeed my legs, which I was trying to keep close together for the sake of a bit of decorum.

The landing was fine, not ungraceful, and overall, I felt exhilarated.

One of the crew helped me with my harness. Henry looked on, being strapped into his.

'Whatever were you doing?' he said to me, mildly reproachfully.

'They were waving. I was trying to follow instructions.'

Henry shook his head.

'But we were just talking, talking about the state of the euro and whether it was f-for good or bad. I think the *marinheiros* – he smiled, almost shyly, at the two sailors, proud of his new word – 'were just gesticulating to pu-punctuate the argument.'

For some reason, I felt very annoyed at that. To get rid of my frustration I took the video camera and made sure that I got shots right up Henry's crutch when he went up, and did funny angles as he came down so that I made him look like one of those dolly pegs, legs tightly together, thighs fat and squashed.

Pathetic, I know, but at the time I felt so cheated: just as I was feeling free as a bird, some idiot had to give me the wrong signals, causing me to redirect not only my activities but my very equilibrium. And then to be told it was *my* fault.

What a fucking liberty.

Our flights complete, we had a great boat ride back to the Marina, and Henry took more film, which seemed inspired at the time as we marvelled at the redness of the sand and rocks, as if they were tinged with blood.

Anyway, we'd had our fun, and when we got off the boat, thanking our sailors profusely, we went off and celebrated with a light meal, just a little salad, and white wine instead of red, and lots of water. From our vantage point outside a sweet little restaurant, we could see the city walls, the old *Fortaleza*, the fort. We spent a good couple of hours there, then we went home.

Henry put the video footage onto the laptop, and we watched it through. I did look majestic flying away, and so did Henry, though I did chuckle at the distorted images of his knees as he came into land, which amused me. The scenic shots didn't look so inspired as when we were taking them, they rarely do. There's the sea, there's a cave, there's the sea, there's a rock, you know the kind of thing, awesome in the moment, but repetitive on film. The naked men in their cove added a little variety and intrigue, and Henry had managed a close-up.

Then we made love, the exhilaration of the day coursing through our veins, I guess. This time Henry managed to hold on until I was satisfied, although once again I must confess to having fantasies to help me reach that point of no return. When we were done, he looked surprisingly far away, unusual for Henry.

'A penny for them,' I invited. I was curious. He looked at me, but still vacantly, like he was not quite plugged in at the wall.

'Sailors,' he said, 'it must be such a free life.'

We showered and had an evening swim then, all in all a great day. Then we went to bed with our books, and before long Henry patted me amicably on my shoulder, turned away from me, sighed and fell into a sleep.

So I crept out of bed, risked another secret cigarette – only my second this week, well done me – and took out the laptop. There was a message on Skype from Rosie, my second daughter, but I decided to address that tomorrow, so here I am updating my blog instead.

I'm ready for a small port now, and then I'll probably get a good night's sleep.

Tchau.

hormones

april 8th 2010

It's the night after the morning before, and what a bloody weird day it's been. It's like living in a book sometimes, life with Henry. Dr Jekyll and Mr Hyde, to be precise. Though who is who isn't always easy to work out.

I woke up full of energy so nipped out for an early morning walk on the beach. It's about two kilometres from here right down to the sands. Our villa is in a terrace, six houses joined together, but all different in style. I think ours is the biggest. It's certainly the only one to have two brass lions at the foot of the drive. We're right on a bend, and all the gardens are walled.

The first kilometre to the village is unspoiled, just the derelict farmhouse opposite, and on the right are hillocks and a narrow road, flanked by aloe vera plants. I'd like to learn to cull them, exploit their goodness right at source. It's all quite lush (apparently there's been a very wet winter this year) and white-walled red-roofed houses dot the horizon. Peaceful.

As I came into the village, the peace was shattered by the sound of dogs barking, loads of them. The first houses you see are the old one storey houses, and the bar, *Ricardo's*, where the Three Wise Monkeys hang out, is on the left opposite a load of green bins. You don't get dustbins for the houses here in Portugal, just communal bins which are emptied daily – much more sensible.

As I turned the bend, I passed a little old lady in black, with bowed, presumably arthritic, knees. She looked to have no teeth, loads of character lines (clearly, no Clarins in the old Portugal), and very sparkly eyes. She nodded at me, and growled a low word. I couldn't quite hear it, so I just said a very cheery 'olá' at her and waved. Then I walked past the paper shop and said hello to João's mother, who was standing in the doorway, smiling and nodding.

Getting to be quite the native☺.

I passed the bus stop where the men sit on the right, then took the right-hand fork to the beach, which sparkled vast and white, fully exposed by a low tide. I breathed in the smell of the sea, its silver hue seeming to shimmer with really strong energies today.

Which sort of goes with the volatile vibes I got later.

I walked briskly up and down the beach four or five times before climbing the steps up to the promontory, then back up the hill. My glutes and buttocks practically screamed at me with gratitude for looking after them so well. Then I smelled the aroma of fresh bread – heaven – nipped again into the *padaria*.

'Bom dia.' The lady with the currant black eyes greeted me with a big smile. 'You are hungry now, yes?' She imitated someone walking briskly, raising her knees in exaggerated fashion.

'Yes,' I smiled, 'yes I am.'

She nodded, and proceeded to choose me four croissants and a loaf of multigrain bread, indicating to me all the while, nodding and pointing. I thanked her, and took home my lovely warm croissants for breakfast.

I made fresh orange juice and took up a tray to Henry, and placed it on his bedside table while I pulled back the curtains. I kissed him on the head, and said into his ear, 'Rise and shine, honey, it's a beautiful day.'

To which he said, 'Oh, for God's sake, Izzie, must you be so sodding cheerful!' And when I said, 'Okay, no need to be stroppy now', he just sat bolt upright, looked at me and shouted, 'Oh my God, don't tell me you're having a menopausal day', and then dived back under the duvet. I was so surprised at how aggressive he was that I gasped, which he must have thought was a sob, because he bounced up again saying, 'And don't do that crying thing, it's so manipulative'.

So much for Henry's win/win attitude that he spouts so much on his bloody training courses. I quietly despised him with my soul and left the grumpy old bastard in bed, came down to get my croissant and made a huge cup of milky coffee to go with it. If anyone's being hormonal today, I thought, it's certainly not me.

Hormones are one of the most powerful aspects of our physiology, aren't they. You know, I've always fancied myself in touch with the biorhythms of life, a woman of the spirit of the moon, or, as a feminist book I once read would have it, a woman who runs with the wolves.

It's not that I don't think moods swing, of course they bloody do. My take is simply that at certain times of the menstrual cycle women merely intensify what is already there. This can be positive as well as negative. I've often regarded myself as more creative as my moon cycle gets nearer, and empowered at the moment of menstruation. Other times, if I happen to be a little fractious round about this time, then so be it. I'm sure that most of the time this has never been a problem to my loved ones.

And if they say it has, then that only goes to show how intolerant they can be.

However, over the last two years, things have changed on the hormonal score for me. At first, it was an almost imperceptible change: a period a bit earlier or later than my usual regular twenty-eight days: a little more pain, a touch more tetchiness. And I began to experience changes in my body temperature, feeling hotter or cooler than Henry, or whoever else I might be near.

Especially at night. On one occasion I woke up to find the bed covered in the aftermath of a very severe sweat. Henry had woken me specially because it was so uncomfortable. I felt mortified. I mean, I'm no prude, but we all know that a healthy glow is more seemly in a woman than a full blown sweat. I can't really claim that sodden sheets could be attributed to a healthy glow. Undoubtedly, this was the work of a proverbial sweating pig.

Which is how Henry began to describe me, checking at night whether I would be 'oinking', as if so he would go in the spare room. I increasingly told him he'd be much better off in the spare room. I don't like the public school elements of his humour, and felt both offended and scornful of his puny pig jokes. Then he'd say that my response was all part of the very hormonal swings of which I speak. I didn't really care by then, because as he flounced out in his dressing gown, I was already enjoying that I got to stay in the best bed.

On my own☺.

Shortly after the onslaught of the sweats, there followed incidents with moods.

One night, I went to bed as normal, Clarins Overnight Skin Restructuring cream carefully applied, the yoga pose of the Plough completed for a good five minutes. I do it a few times a week, to stimulate my thyroid gland.

With hindsight, maybe bedtime isn't a good time to stimulate things, because on that occasion I think I inadvertently triggered production of just a little too much thyroxin, unleashing a level of hyperactivity in the mental sphere.

I had a restless night, and, to my utter surprise, woke the next morning in tears. I was thinking about Stefan, and how much I missed him, and wondering if he was okay; and then I got to thinking about the other three, and whether or not I had been a

Good Mother. I believe fully in Winnicott's concept of the 'good enough mother', yet it just didn't help me on that day. I *should* have been better, I *should* have made life easy for them all, but I didn't, I just bloody well didn't. I considered my inadequacies, told myself that I'm a better mum than some and worse than others, rationalised that their fathers all had their part to play. My mind was busy with realization that, navel gazing apart, there is a part of me which just misses all my children, in an everyday sense.

I felt an unspeakable longing. I knew that if I voiced it to Henry, he'd only give me platitudes of 'you have to let them go', and so on, which would miss the point. I *can* let them go, and I have. I was just realizing that sometimes I miss the times when they were little, and medium size, and we were close, and there was something animal, something wonderful there that I didn't get any more. So platitudes would never have done.

Who was it who said that although there's more to being a woman then being a mother, there's a hell of a lot more to being a mother than most people suspect?

Perhaps it was me.

Anyway, there they were, these maternal thoughts, and I felt a sudden and profound sense of loss, which progressed to a feeling of Void. Who would miss me if I weren't here? What contribution had I ever made to the great scheme of things? What could I do to effect world famine? What excitement had I to look forward to that weekend? Would anyone ever whistle at me in the street again?

Of course, these thoughts weren't arranged as neatly as I describe them. Rather, they popped haphazardly into my head between masses of tears.

When I surfaced from my watery bed, and staggered self-pityingly to the mirror, my features mocked me from beneath the deflating balloon which used to be my skin. That morning marked the beginning of a period in which I felt compelled to look more frequently than ever in the mirror, searching my eyes for someone who I was sure used to be in there, but who had clearly vacated the corporeal premises.

Then came sensitivity. I took umbrage at the slightest remark. For example when Henry accused me of being forgetful, I hit the roof. Henry denied using accusative tones, but I *felt* accused, and if I *felt*, therefore I was (no wonder I had got on so well with Stig the lovely philosopher, I'm a natural). Henry alleged that I had thrown away some papers regarding an important client. The distressing thing was that I couldn't remember if I had or not, whereas at one time my memory was razor sharp.

Typical of Henry to leave them all over the house for days at a time, cluttering up my space into the bargain, and blocking all the chi energy which I really believe is essential to a healthy environment.

So when he made the accusation, I burst into tears. I proceeded to yell at him, and told him to 'fuck off, you boring old suit', which I afterwards regretted. Henry *can* seem dull at times, but then his dependability is the very quality that I like. Surely it's unfair of me to want dependable *and* interesting?

Surely.

I digress: the point is that I suddenly found myself teetering on the edge of a chasm of despair. I fell into a habit of reviewing whole episodes from my past. I discovered feelings of primal rage regarding things that had happened twenty, thirty, or even forty years ago. I'm ashamed to say that there were whole moments when I truly hated Mother, remembering her as insensitive and cold, when I needed her to be cuddly and warm. I regularly felt both hatred and longing for my barely known father, who failed to survive to see me grow up. My sense of abandonment felt huge, my sense of loneliness profound. There were sudden bouts of unpredictable hostility and teary vilification. I would shout at people (well, mostly Henry, actually) for no apparent reason (other than that they/he were really getting on my nerves). We agreed that the hostility was irrational (though I can feel myself wanting to argue with that analysis, so maybe my hormones are swinging as we speak).

I found light at the end of the menopausal tunnel when I accepted that resistance was futile. I began to embrace the volatile uncertainty of what it is to be me, even to revel in discovering the monster within. I learned to enjoy feeling stroppy. I not only shouted at Henry, I extended my range of victims to anyone who got my goat. In fact I deliberately put my goat out to be got – I was evil.

Once I fully acknowledged this, I felt a certain freedom to behave as I liked, with a liberating 'fuck you' attitude never far from reach.

One of my first menopausal triumphs was with the bank manager at HSBC who had the cheek to bounce a cheque, just because I had forgotten to pay in funds to cover my direct debits.

I was incensed. I had been a client of hers for nigh on thirty years, and this was the first time ever that anything had gone wrong.

She wrote to me, emphasizing the need to 'ensure that you have sufficient funds to cover debits', as if I was some kind of imbecile. (I feel annoyed even thinking about it – did I take my agnus castus this morning?). I considered my reply carefully, and can recall it practically verbatim.

Dear Ms Mackay,

Thank you so much for your recent correspondence regarding my account.

I realize that it would be unreasonable for me to have expected you to honour my direct debits for the beginning of this month which have, after all, only been going out of my account, without fail for the last twenty-seven years. Never mind that I have a savings account with you (healthy, I might add, to a sum thirty times that of the debits which were due to be made), and two ISAs. I can see that none of these factors mean that you can trust me. And my end of month cheques have only going in on a regular basis for that same twenty-seven years, or, let's see now, 324 times without fail.

I realize that it would have been too much effort for you to have telephoned me to discuss the situation. Naturally your time is better spent calculating the very reasonable charges of twenty pounds per recalled direct debit.

I am just a humble customer. Some might say I am part of a collective who actually employ you, and who, between us, pay your bloody salary. And that our money enables your bosses bloody bankers' bonuses. Some might say that we should be respected.

But no. You are right, I am wrong. I really should realize that sufficient funds need to be in my account if I expect direct debits to be honoured.

Well, thank you for pointing that out. I have now stood in the corner of my office with a dunce's cap on for an hour, so I think that I have been punished enough, and I will try to Do Better in future.

Yours, faithfully (twenty-seven years worth, actually)

Izzie Childs   PhD. MA. MEd

Ms McKay telephoned me some days later, with a note of concern in her voice. By then I was through the worst of the uphill stint on my emotional roller coaster. I accepted her apology and got the charges refunded. Then I changed my banking arrangements by taking my custom to the Co-op – so much more ethical.

There was a real energy in that little episode. I realised that my anger was quite appropriate, and that, far from being 'not very nice', as Attila always said, was liberating. Certainly better than depression: I read somewhere that some psychologists define certain types of depression as anger turned inwards. So it really was much healthier in the long run for me to give evil Izzie some rein, and I settled into the license that my hormones afforded me.

Though I drew the line at a friend's suggestion that 'now you'll be able to go shoplifting, and then blame it on your hormones'.

I have approached shopping, however, in a different way, with the odd incident here and there. About a year ago, for example, I was out with dear old Jutta, looking round a posh dress shop, wondering what to try on for the hell of it, when we noticed a young man and woman having words. It went something like this:

He: Whinge, whinge, whinge. Can we go yet?
She: Oh do stop whingeing (fondles lovely silk blouse).
He: Whinge, whinge, whinge. The football's on soon.
She (irritated, letting silk blouse fall from her fingers): Oh for goodness sake, if you don't want to be in here, just go and wait outside.
He (provocatively): What's up with you, on your period or something? You sound like my mum.
She: (looks embarrassed and deflated, begins to walk away from lovely clothes)

I decided to intervene.

(Enter the Evil One, stage right).

EO (sweetly): Well if you didn't behave so much like a child, she wouldn't *have* to sound like your mummy, would she?

(Jutta looks aghast, as does man. Woman looks startled.)

EO (smiling sweetly at man): So sorry, it must have been my hormones. At least I'll be nice again in five minutes. What's your excuse?

(Exit Evil One, stage left, winks at woman who is chuckling)

A mixed bag, these hormones, all in all☺.

One downside is that once labelled menopausal, every difference, every cross word is then interpreted by loved ones (yes, again, I mostly mean Henry) as being attributable to hormones. Whenever we mis-communicate he sees it as my fault, which is unfair. It's a bit like being diagnosed as mad: once labelled, everything you do is seen through that filter. I'm sure if men had menopauses they would design some kind of annual menopause leave to accommodate the changes. And I'm sure that if we laughed at the changes that occur for *them* or groaned at the inconvenience that many women describe as testosterone decreases and men lose hair or sexual performance, or if I laughed at poor Henry's stutter, (and believe me I think that hormone regulation is just as uncontrollable an issue) then that would be seen as cruel.

Double standards. But there you go.

Once I'd mentally revisited the History of my Hormones with my coffee and croissant while Henry snored away his bad karma, I lay on the sunbed until he got up and came and made me tea. No reference to his ugly mood of earlier, just gesture enough to let me know that he knows he was out of order.

Later, we went on a ride out to explore the pottery shops, which proliferate along the roadsides in the Algarve. I bought two big wall plates, which depict scenes of labourers in fields, surrounded by fruit, trees, and animals.

Actually, they are hideous, and Henry hates them. I just couldn't resist exploiting his guilt and his need to be sycophantic. I am resolved to make him carry them home in his hand luggage, as well☺.

To my utter amazement, it rained from late afternoon onwards, stair rods, a real downpour. I hadn't expected that for this time of year. I replied to Rosie's e-mail, and got on with reading my novel, until the sun broke out again. Henry suggested dinner out, but I was in no mood to go and play Mr and Mrs, so we had a drink on the terrace early evening.

Blow me, if we weren't joined by Joe and his helpmate, who turns out to be Russian, and called Vlad. Apparently they'd been just passing, and so had come to see if everything was okay (even though they'd only been two days ago, by my reckoning).

We gave them a beer, and it was good fun, me harbouring my sexual fantasies, Henry fawning and seeming to get on well enough with both lads. It lifted our spirits. So now we've both snapped out of our respective moods, and he's in the shower and we're going down the road for a drink. Henry has already got a little tipsy with the lads, and I noticed when he went to the bathroom that he was talking to himself, words that sounded like 'fuck you, f-f-f-f-f-ather, just fuck you.'

I didn't ask – I was just pleased he could manage two fucks without a stutter.

oxford dons

april 9th 2010

I think I might have made my mark in the village.

We walked down all the way to the beach, beneath lovely skies washed clean by the rain, and a gentle sunset. We had a bit of a mooch and then settled on one of the local hostelries, *O Pescador*, which means the fisherman. It's quite English looking, an old-fashioned wooden bar with mirrors behind, heavy beams across the ceiling held up by massive posts here and there. The seats are made out of small barrels, with a cushion dropped on, although there are benches around as well, and of course, stools for the barflies. It's quite dim, though there are some fairy lights hung here and there, and small candles on the tables.

There were about nine or ten people in I suppose, so we sat at a bar stool and had a large gin and tonic each – and I mean *large*. Henry was vibrant, far removed from the dark mood that he had cast earlier. We chatted to the barmen, each accomplished multi-taskers, serving and making social patter, flashing white teeth and interested eyes our way.

We got talking to another couple, Claudia and Matt. She is Portuguese and he is English, they both live in Oxford, and will stay in England apparently while their children are growing up.

I know Oxford really well. As it happens, it's where I conceived Jon, my eldest son.

The weirdest coincidence occurred, just as we finished our second drink. We were well engaged with Claudia and Matt. Matt is in Human Resources, right up Henry's street, and Claudia is a working mum, running her own eco-friendly nappy company from home, which she calls greenbabbikins.com, very clever. The bar had filled up behind us. Suddenly, out of the blue, I heard raucous laughter and a broad Midlands accent.

'Oh, come on Nuno, let's have the music up a bit, ey, we can't hardly hear it!' A cheer went up, and I turned around to see about four people dancing in the middle of the floor. And guess what, one of them was the Thornton Tart from the plane.

And she was having a ball.

She was wearing the brightest outfit you could imagine, a jumpsuit of all things, in rainbow colours and with shoestring straps. Her chubby little body looked surprisingly good, big smiley face, nice tan, and her backside was curvaceous. I had to stop myself staring at first, and was amazed as she began to perform a tongue in cheek pole dance around the middle post of the wooden infrastructure.

Suddenly, I couldn't help myself, I was up there with them, dancing to Barry White, carried away on a burst of spontaneity.

TT gave me a smile, so I went over at the end of the dance, and said, 'I know you from the plane, d'you remember? I'm Izzie.'

But she didn't. Remember me, I mean. While I had been being so critical, and obsessed with trivia, clearly she was just going about her business. Turns out her name is Jean, and she lives in the Algarve, going back to the UK now and then to work there and supplement her income. Her family is over, that's why she was out on the town.

I left her to it, feeling that pang of envy again as she laughed and danced away. I wondered when I'd ever got so bloody self-righteous.

And ordered my third – *large* – gin and tonic.

Claudia congratulated me on dancing, and then asked me how I knew Oxford so well. My tongue was quite loose now, so I told her.

'My son Jon's father was at Oxford. Marc. I met him at Glastonbury. We were sitting smoking dope in a field. T. Rex were playing on a nearby stage that we couldn't be arsed to move to see. We thought we were dead cool, you know how it is.' Claudia nodded. In the cold light of day, I wonder if she would have any clue as to 'how it is'. She's a bit younger than me, and anyway, did the Portuguese youth of the seventies do the same as us?

I rabbited on.

'Marc was hot. Tall, long dark hair in a headband, brown eyes, slim hipped. He had this fab voice, you know, like liquid sex, very posh accent.'

Claudia looked a little perplexed, but that didn't stop me.

'But he wasn't poncey, really, just more kind of perfect.'

Truth was, I knew I would sleep with Marc as soon as our arms touched and an electric current passed between us. I shivered a little at the memory.

'Anyway, Claudia, turned out he was reading Classics. By the end of the night, he was telling me about the stars, as we lay side by side in the glow of a camp fire. Did you know how the Greeks named their gods, Claudia?'

Claudia said no, and shuffled in her seat, looking at me intensely.

'Did you know that the father of the gods, Claudia, is not Zeus?'

'No, Izzie, I did not.' She sipped her drink, looked nervously around.

'Neither did I. Anyway, finally I just rolled over onto him and asked if he would mind if I shagged him. Have you ever done that, Claudia?'

I took a large sip of my gin, and remember thinking that Claudia looked a bit blurred around the edges. I wondered if she'd had too much to drink. I might have wondered it out loud.

Claudia coughed, and I think it was around then that I nearly dropped my glass while trying to straighten my posture. I noticed that Matt had come nearer and had his arm around Claudia's shoulders. She looked slightly alarmed. I made an effort.

'Of course, *your* stars are wonderfully bright, too, aren't they – we always notice that, don't we Henry?' I looked around me for support, but Henry was by now engrossed in conversation with the barman. Before I knew it, Claudia and Matt were saying cheerio and I was at Henry's side, ordering more gin.

Next thing I remember was Henry walking me home, underneath those very lovely stars, and I remember giggling a lot and belting out a rendition of *The Black Hills of Dakota*. When we got home I insisted on a midnight swim, very refreshing.

Today I feel slightly fuzzy. Shit, actually. I've had some fresh orange juice and a bit of a doze, and Henry has gone off for a walk on his own. I'm just sitting here thinking.

About Marc.

He didn't, of course, mind – me shagging him, that is. Almost shagging, at any rate. I had no contraception, and neither did he, and I was mindful of the lovely Constantine at home with Attila. So I wouldn't go all the way, just nearly, with the excitement that comes with a certain amount of forbidden entry.

Leaving us wanting more.

I couldn't dare tell Attila that I fancied myself in love, and I couldn't take extra weekends away from Con. Marc and I stayed in touch by letter and a very occasional phone call.

In the Autumn term, I hitchhiked up to Oxford from Uni. Marc was as hot as I remembered, and we spent a lot of time in bed, finishing what we'd started. Oxford was something else. The college was truly awesome, boasting gorgeous courtyards, riddled with staircases, nooks and crannies. Marc's room was enormous, huge windows set in stone walls, and had its own bathroom. He had a daily cleaner, who they called a scout. Talk about a different world.

I insisted that we go on the river, so we put big woolly jumpers on and hired a punt. We saw deer. I was very excited, I'd never seen deer in Birmingham. We passed the house where C.S. Lewis used to live. It was magical.

We snatched secret meetings when we could. Christmas apart was excruciatingly difficult. Connie was eighteen months now. Already she was a strangely 'good' girl. I would enthusiastically roll on the floor playing with her new Pooh Bear while she clapped encouragingly. It was me who got the finger paints out and made a mess in the bathroom by doing foot and toe prints, and it was Connie who stayed clean. She kept on dabbing at me with a well wrung out flannel whenever I had paint on me, and freaked out if she had any on her hand. I felt like something was badly awry when we ended up with two great pictures of my feet and my hands, but none of hers. I fancied a bit of a chill around her sometimes. When she recited her numbers, which she could already do perfectly, it was no surprise to me that she repeated the number six three times, and thought that to be very funny.

When I got back to Uni, I saw Marc at every possible opportunity, for a whole year. We shagged all over his rooms, on the stairwell, in the deer park (chilly in March, idyllic nonetheless) and then, in the summer, on a punt in the river.

Literally *in* the river by the time we finished.

I loved Marc to bits, but the odds were stacked against us. I was an unmarried mother, a bit of a trollop, and he an Oxford scholar. He assured me that when he went to study at the prestigious Italian university for his Masters it would be okay, we'd find a way round it.

Then, blow me, didn't I find out I was pregnant.

It came as a shock. I thought it must have been the night of the May Ball. I'd hitched up for the weekend, and had a bit of a dodgy encounter with a lorry driver. Usually I got some old geezer who had a daughter the same age as me who picked me up so that a pervert didn't, that kind of thing. But with this one, I think he picked me up *because* he had a daughter the same age as me, and *was* the pervert.

Oops.

I managed to run off from him at a services near Reading, pretext of toilet, and then got a lift to the railway station to finish my journey in safety. I was shaken up and began to drink on the train. Once I got to Oxford and met up with Marc we drank more, long into the night. I spent the whole of the morning of the May ball with my head down the toilet, losing not only all the alcohol, but all the hormonal benefit of my Microgynon 30.

On the afternoon of the ball, we began again. The tutors provided drinks on the lawns for the third year students. From three o'clock onwards we were out there eating canapés (a new experience for me, sausages on sticks and a chunk of cheese and pineapple were more the rage in my previous life) and drinking real champagne, with a string quartet playing in the background. At some point Marc grabbed my hand and took me inside one of the old buildings, all the way up the stairs until we came out on the roof halfway up Magdalen college tower (stunning view). We were shagging within minutes. Some second years got wind and looked out of the window at us, congratulating our ardour and sending out plastic cups full of champagne to keep us going.

Thus, I assume, dear Jon was conceived.

So finals came and went and there I was, pregnant again. Marc was pragmatic. He and his family would naturally support me and the baby financially, but he really did have to go on to study in Italy, which apparently I'd hate. We stayed friends for a while, even lovers until the distance between his elitist world and my very practical one became too great. I took a year off and moved back home, working part-time in a playgroup, then I was accepted on my teacher training course. My fate was cast. Marc eventually became a senior politician, in fact now he's in the Cabinet. He's provided well for Jon, including sending him through public school.

I wonder now if it was hard for Jon to be the product of two such different cultures. I don't see him often, but when I do he seems to be having a good time (even if his pupils are a little more dilated than the norm). He is successful in what he does, something in the world of finance. I realise, to my shame, I don't even know precisely what that something is.

Henry and I are going to go to a local fish restaurant tonight, a little way up the coast. We've ordered a taxi so that we can both drink. Henry's loving the red wine. He has also, to my great surprise, begun to smoke a little here and there, which is most odd as he is such a stickler about the health and hygiene issues to do with smoking. He's acquired some rolling tobacco and some liquorice papers, I think from Vlad who was apparently in the bar last night, though I didn't notice him. Henry used to smoke roll-ups back in the day, and has just rediscovered the fancy. So he's certainly chilling out.

Tomorrow we both have a bit of an indulge session booked in at the local Spa. Not long now until Jutta arrives, with Tammi, so we're beginning the countdown for the party. Overall, I'm looking forward to it, or at least the idea of it.

Age is funny, isn't it, because it's just another year, yet you put an 0 on the end of a birthday and then suddenly you're taking stock. If we didn't know our dates of birth, I wonder how differently we might mark out our lives.

dream on

april 10th 2010

I had a wonderful dream last night, you know those ones where you can feel every sensation, smell each smell, almost taste the atmosphere. I dreamed that one of my daughters, not sure which at first, was with an older woman, a woman of Asian extraction, someone who I just knew was very wise. She was dressed in a turquoise sari, and had a crystal hanging on her forehead where the bindhi usually is on Sikh women. She smelled of incense and something less exotic, like Vaseline underarm deodorant. She wore walking sandals, and I had the impression that she could trek for hours, even with someone on her back, if necessary.

The vague daughter was smiling, and said that she was making some major changes in her life. Then I realised it was Connie, because she had an awful hairdo but was really quite pretty underneath, and she seemed to be divesting herself of garments, even as I watched. There was a strange hazy bit because when she divested, she sort of threw her garments into the air where they got sucked into a space tunnel, and I'm sure that she threw a couple of young children in there too, and was seeming very happy about this. She hugged me closely and I knew that all the angst and distance between us was gone, and that she really was becoming the vibrant person who I always knew to be hidden inside her.

It was a lovely feeling, because I've always loved her deeply, despite our complex relationship. So I take the dream to be some kind of portent, even though later in the dream, I was in a large building and experiencing an earthquake, floors shaking and the view from the window tipping this way and that.

I don't know what Freud, or indeed Atilla, would make of that one. Curiously enough, over the last few months or so, I sometimes *am* aware of a kind of trembly sensation beneath me, or a slight sense of swaying, when I'm fully awake. Perhaps it's a mild kind of vertigo. It's bewildering, and no doubt *you know who* would attribute it to the menopause, so I haven't told anyone.

Maybe it was the fish last night that set off the dream. The food was lovely at the restaurant that we went to, out towards Sagres somewhere, but it was rich. We got talking to a couple from

Brussels, they have a 'place' here, in a village called Figueira, and they were talking about why they love to visit but wouldn't live here. It's too narrow a culture, they said. Maybe they're right, though for now the place just seems a haven of light and luxury to *me.

Anyway, we ended up having an uneventful night, and so this morning rose feeling quite fresh, and off Henry and I went to the Spa, as promised. I decided to go for yoga, to ground myself after these contrasting dreams, and I definitely did that. Most of the exercise today was to open the hips and knees. I was mostly fine, though felt the pull when I went into the pose of the grasshopper, and to be honest, as far as I'm concerned, the damned grasshopper can keep his poses to himself. I did yoga throughout my second and third pregnancies, enhancing the natural childbirth process. I was very supple. I have photos of me taken all the way through, naked pregnant woman does yoga. I thought it avant-garde.

I tend to keep the photos to myself now, as I wonder who really is that interested in a naked woman doing yoga. Naked pregnant woman at that.

I digress: the yoga teacher, Ana, was svelte, bum like a pumpkin and the most beautifully straight back. She also does hypnotism, so I might go and see her after my party to see if she can help me quit smoking. Even the odd one is definitely exacerbating the lines around my mouth and chin. Ana emphasized that no one must do more than they are capable of.

'You are not in competition.' Her voice was soft yet authoritative. 'You must remember that in yoga, the mental state is as important as the physical.'

I listened intently, but couldn't help but glance out of the corner of my eye to see how the others were doing, and found myself stretching that teensy-weensy bit extra to try to complete to the full posture. Forward bends were difficult, more from an unseemly point of view as much as anything else, those little rolls around the middle becoming larger by the second. I wanted to grab hold of them and pull them from my body.

Not really very karmic, I suppose.

The other thing which I find a bit embarrassing in yoga classes, and always have, is that when I do an inverted posture, particularly the Plough, not only does my stomach seem to increase in girth and slide down and hit me in the face, but air sometimes escapes from my vagina with a triumphant whoosh.

76

Is this normal, would you say?

It's a real effort to control these fanny farts. I do sometimes manage, but if one does escape, what *is* the etiquette? Should you justify yourself with a loud explanation that it's not really a fart, but a vaginal leak? And if so, is that any less embarrassing? Today, it just happened once, quite lightly, and I simply smiled to myself and pretended it wasn't me.

I felt well stretched by the end of the session. Then I went to a beauty therapist who gave me a facial, Clarins super-duper rejuvenation and line reducer. After an hour and a quarter of cleansing, creaming and massaging, my skin felt radiant. Then I had a sea salt scrub and body rub, followed by immersion in a float tank, and I felt fabulous. When Henry met me at the appointed hour, I was nearly asleep on my sunbed in the shade near the pool.

'You look gorgeous,' he said, and held out his hand to help me up.

'So do you,' I said, and meant it. He smelled of some kind of sports rub mix, and looked really relaxed. We sauntered hand in hand to the car, and drove off through the spa complex, past the golf course where we'd played with that awful couple, Fred and Antonia. Was that really only a week ago? It seems like forever.

We headed down through ornamental gardens, which reminded me of those miniature gardens you used to get when you were small, all bright green turf and perfect walled flowerbeds. We opted for Salema again, which is located down a very steep hill, edged with telegraph poles, and peppered with tiny hamlets which pop out at certain points. There are camper vans everywhere. Some are the real old authentic VWs, and we noticed several of those on the drive of a German complex which seemed to be offering something *naturisto*, as well as regular camping. Some were more winnibagoes, out of which you might expect a grinning Jack Nicholson to emerge at any moment. Henry got excited by how many hooper birds we saw with their brown and white stripes, and I was intrigued by the graffiti which appears with regularity on some of the older more derelict buildings.

Once we'd snaked down the road to the village, we parked up and breathed the sea air on the recently renovated seafront, cobbles prevalent on road and promenade. An old toothless woman offered us lace. I took Henry's hand in mine.

'I love you Henry Chamberlain!' I screamed, and gave him a great hug and a kiss, and in that moment my spirit moved with the rhythm of the waves.

We mooched around to find a restaurant, up a little road with an African shop, through a little alley down to the beach, and walked along the sand past the fishing boats which were full of lobster pots and fishing nets. One of the houses on the front was for sale, with permission to build up on it. We wondered whether it would really be good to live there, to follow the dream. Henry decided that the noise of the sea would be too relentless, and not all it was cracked up to be. I thought about what that couple had said last night.

We stumbled upon a small café right on the beach, and sat outside, the salty smell of the ocean assailing our senses. We ordered salads and water to keep up our feeling of wellness, and chatted about this and that. Henry was unusually communicative, especially after he got a text from James. He looked at it inquisitively.

'F-father,' he said, and then had to go inside to read it as the light outside was too bright to be able to see the screen. My heart sank as I hoped it wasn't another of those stupid memos.

When he came out, Henry sat down and looked me in the eye.

'I have some news,' he said, 'and I don't really know if it's good news or bad.'

I raised an eyebrow.

'It's Mother and F-father,' he said, 'they've been trapped in the volcanic ash cloud.'

The volcanic ash cloud. We'd heard a couple near us talking about their flight, which was supposed to be tonight, and how it had been cancelled. But we haven't really been looking at the news, so are a bit out of touch with the state of things with the airport.

'Trapped?' I stifled a giggle, enjoying images of James stuffy Chamberlain stopped in his tracks for once, by something that, finally, even he couldn't control.

'Yes.' Henry looked like he didn't quite know which expression he wanted to wear, as if he was holding back. 'They're in the States, you know, and were due to fly back today. Then they were going to come over to Faro tomorrow and spend a w-week at Quinta da Lago and then surprise you f-for your birthday.'

A shiver ran down me. Prepare to hang out the garlic.

'But now it looks like they can't get a flight back to the UK for at least three days, so everything is thrown into limbo. And he's got some business at the office as one of the other MDs has been stuck in Germany for a couple of days. So it seems there's some doubt as to whether they'll be able to come.'

Henry was, I noticed now, speaking with a calmness and a fluency that surprised me.

'You don't sound too upset?' I ventured, stifling a loud *woohoo*, just in case I had it wrong.

He looked pensive.

'Well, you know, maybe it might be better if they weren't here. It's kind of nice relaxing without them, a bit of a chance to be myself.' He blushed slightly. 'I've been thinking a lot of things this holiday.'

I was intrigued, but just then the salad arrived, and Henry turned his attention to thank the waitress. We ate, and chilled, and I said a silent prayer to the Universe. I was surprised at how liberating it felt, the thought of that stuffy old goat and prim old matron not being here at my party, and felt really chuffed that Henry thought so too.

A lovely day. A quiet evening in for us with a film, I think, to maximize the detox effects of our wonderful morning. I've planned a quiet day tomorrow too, and then a trip out for Henry on Thursday before the first arrivals, a surprise to thank him for my surprise.

Good times.

wondering what I want

april 11th 2010

Well we had our lovely quiet evening, smoothies under the stars, and then watched a film, *The Bucket List* with Jack Nicholson and Morgan Freeman, all about what you might want to do if you were given a terminal diagnosis. It got me thinking. Henry didn't say much more about anything, and I know better than to ask him. He's quite private, is Henry. We have a bit of a rub along relationship really, come to think of it, I suppose we probably both spend quite a lot of time in our own heads, but that seems pretty comfortable to me.

Comfortable. A good state to be in at my age. Much better than drama, or too much intensity.

So a lazy late get up today, fresh orange juice on the terrace, and settled down on the sunbed. At around ten o'clock, just as I was lying in the shade reading my Rose Tremaine book, I heard a truck pull up, and yes, it was the pool men again. Joe was back, with Vlad, both smiling and greeting us in a really friendly way. My heart rate went up just a little bit, and I waved, tipping my hat down slightly over my eyes so that I could appear enigmatic. They brought in their equipment and started on their jobs. I noticed that Henry was very chatty, standing with them as they brushed the sides of the pool and put in the huge vacuum pipes. He looked uncharacteristically manly I thought, and is getting quite a tan. I tried not to watch too obtrusively. Henry went and fetched some beers. I didn't have one, a bit early in the day for me. Instead I lay supine on the sunlounger, breathing tightly in and out to make my stomach a strong core, revelling in what I imagined to be an enigmatic posture.

Unfortunately, and maybe because I was still carrying the deep relaxation of yesterday, I fell asleep and only realised that I had when I awoke to the sound of my own little snore. The lads were all chuckling about something when I came to, so I think I got away with it.

Anyway, it was great to hear dear old Henry mixing so well with the locals. As I say, he may not be the most dynamic of men on first acquaintance, and yes, there are times when I find him boring; and at other times I get that shouting urge, when he is a little passive and has to be organised, reassured or mopped up after. Overall though, he works hard to please me, and has been very good to my offspring, and, in fact, to Mother. He is reasonable looking, his income is satisfactory, and now he has been a complete sweetheart and organised this fabulous surprise for me.

So what more could a woman ask for, really?

The answer is that I don't know, but I think there might be something. Looking back over various bits and bobs in my life, I think I've done well to get to where I am. Yet when I reminisce, as of late, I wonder where the woman I used to be has gone, that character who's feisty, who takes risks, who's so *alive*. Truth be told, I miss passion.

And then I look at Joe, and can't work out if I'm just being daft or if I owe it to myself to have a bit more of that passion in my life.

Just one, teensy-weensy, little adventure.

I shook myself, got up, deliberately not holding in my core anymore, trying to be mature for once, and went in and got myself some iced water. When I came out, Joe came over to me.

'Morning, Izzie,' he said, cool as cucumber, 'how are you enjoying your stay then? Good night in the Pescador the other night?'

I felt myself blush. He'd seen me then, frightening the locals with my lewd stories.

'Yes, it was fun. Is it always like that?'

'Only in season.' He grinned at me, a lovely open grin. 'The tourists like to have a bit of a drink.'

I suddenly desperately wanted not to be a tourist.

He went on.

'You guys are here for a good spell. That must be nice – give you a chance to look around.'

'Yes.' I was grateful for the diversion. 'It's a great area.'

'Spectacular natural park around here. Great for walking.'

'Yes, I'd heard. I like walking, actually.'

'There's a walking group, you know, have a look in the local press.' He nodded toward the book on my sunbed. 'I see you read a lot – very relaxing.'

I think he was about to ask something more, when suddenly we both turned as Henry and Vlad guffawed at something, and Henry patted Vlad on the back. Joe raised an eyebrow.

'Better get going. We've loads to do yet. See you next time.'

And he was gone, leaving my molecules slightly disturbed. I felt wrong-footed as I waited for the chlorine to settle in the pool before I could dive in and do my lengths. Then I felt a bit calmer, and thought maybe my hormones were doing their thing. I've got too much time on my hands to think.

So, if I'm going to be thinking too much, I might as well make it useful, and get some kind of focus. I should maybe think about the future. In *Psychologies,* the resident coach was asking some pertinent questions this month, and what with that and my birthday and last night's film, maybe this is an opportunity to really think about what I want. Henry is guzzling another beer now, and is reading a book on ancient Greek culture. He looks content. A perfect time for me to reflect.

So, what lies ahead in the next thirty or forty years? (Clearly, desperately hoping that ninety will be the new fifty-five☺.) Where do I want to go to, and what do I want to achieve? Fenella once reminded me how *Alice In Wonderland* gets stuck in the tunnel with a choice of four exits. The White Rabbit finds her crying and tells her that it doesn't much matter which direction to take if she doesn't know where she's going. Loads of the New Age psychologists use this metaphor, does that mean that Lewis Carroll was really an early life coach, his stories the narrative of quintessential self-discovery?

So the secret, apparently, is to know what you *want*, and to know exactly what that looks like. Keep your list to seven things plus or minus two, Fenella says, so you can remember them. Then, if you start to focus on these things, you might find ways to get them.

So I went through this exercise of asking myself various questions, and it seems that these are the five things I really want.

1. *Happiness.* Goes without saying really, doesn't it. What does that look like? Well, I think if I were happy, I'd smile a lot. I would also experience a deep sense of awe at times, find something new to marvel at. I'd probably do a lot of travel, like this holiday, but also something really adventurous like walking in Nepal. That would be invigorating. I loved it when I walked the Inca Trail, and found it amazing getting into the practicalities; I took face creams in small pots and carried baby wipes for physiological needs, and you know what, one of the great things

was spending a week without looking in a mirror or even thinking of looking in a mirror, liberated from the tyranny of narcissism.

2. *Feeling worthwhile.* I think I would do Good Causes. Maybe build some kind of home for young people who have strayed off the pathway a bit, or maybe somewhere for young immigrant mums, or mums-to-be. It's hard on them. I could be a great patron, the Isabella Childs Trust or something – very fitting name.

It would be great to do something humble like that.

3. *Feeling really fulfilled.* Aah. Now then. In which areas? Sexual fulfilment has to be important, doesn't it? I'm lucky to have had my share of that, and still do. Maybe Tantric sex would enhance things in that department a little. Must make a mental note to self, investigate the local Buddhist centre for starters. I think Henry would be adept at standing on his head, particularly if he thought it might help invigorate his gonads.

On a more serious note, there's more to life than sex, and to be fulfilled I think I would want to have achieved something personal. *And*, I'm enjoying writing this, so perhaps there is a novelist in me waiting to get out. Maybe I'll investigate going on a writing course, one of those Arvon foundation centres or something.

4. *Relationships.* Tricky.

As I said, I'm blessed, really. Of course I would like my relationship with Henry to flourish on and on. Ideally, I would like him to retire soon so that we could have more time together to travel. Although I could do that I suppose with my women friends, who are of utmost importance to me, more so as time passes. I never really valued my women friends when I was younger. I socialised with women intermittently, when it suited me I suppose, at playgroup or on a course or whatever. Jutta was the first great friend, and I've known her twenty-odd years. And Tammi, now she was a find, we were on the same creative cookery course in the wilds of Devon, full of lamb and clotted cream. They are both very important to me and I want to see more of them in the future.

And the children. I'd like to feel that I knew them better, and they me, after all, why on earth bother with having them, otherwise? On the other hand, they only come through you, as Kahil Gabrain so wisely says, they're not really yours, so I'm happy if I know that they are okay, and don't want to crowd them. There are ups and downs, but really I respect all of them, otherwise

I wouldn't care, would I, or even *want* to spend time with them. They're all bright, they're all interesting.

I'm just not sure they're all happy.

And then there's my mother. Atilla. I can be so mean about her, yet she's amazing, and has been a bedrock for me. I know I've taken her for granted. Of late, I find I want to understand her more, and gain some of her womanly wisdom. I wonder what she was thinking when she was coming up to fifty, way before it was the new thirty. I have always thought of her as old, yet that seems wrong now.

5. *Health.* Naturally, I want to live a long and fit life. I think that means all the usual stuff: I have to exercise regularly, give up smoking, and indulge more in therapeutic treatments. People have asked me what gift I would like for my birthday. With body in mind, I've asked for practical things like a workout outfit, a skipping rope (pop it in a bag with your Pilates exercise band and you're away), and some little hand weights for those days when it's hard to get to the gym. I'm doing okay there really.

Maybe I'll just shut up about my health and my habits, because to be honest, I'm in danger of losing the *will* to live if I keep on ruminating about the *way* to live.

In fact, all this fannying around with what you want seems suddenly depressing. I'd rather think about what I want to *do*.

And the truth is that I want to hang on to Henry, and I want to bonk Joe. I want to be really healthy, and I want to drink like a fish, eat like a pig, slob around and smoke like a trooper. I want to be a lazy old sod, and yet achieve great things, walk the world and have a bestselling novel that has written itself. I want to let all my kids be grown-ups and I still want to look after them, and go and do something amazing together.

And there you have it. Total confusion. So much for this bloody life coaching business.

So where does that leave us? Well, the 'us' that is me and Henry have one more day alone before everything changes. And tomorrow is Henry's treat day from me, and he deserves my full attention. I'm taking him on a surprise trip. I think he will just love it. So for the rest of today, I'm going to get myself together, and enjoy each moment.

I see that the geckoes are out, climbing up the walls with those little sucker feet, seeing the world from all ways round and upside down.

84

Now then, *that's* a trick I'd like to be able to do.
I wonder where you can buy those feet?

os golfinhos

april 12th 2010

My little surprise for Henry went swimmingly☺.

    We woke at eightish, which was laid-back and relaxing, and spent a leisurely hour drinking tea in bed. I got up to make it, feeling that I should be giving pampering today and that Henry should be spoiled a little. I took the opportunity to make myself a lemon and hot water detox drink and sip it gently while walking around the garden. There are some lovely plants here – bougainvillea of course, always reliable, huge chunks of shocking pink and brightest purples draping themselves over the garden wall. Then some well tended flower beds (although I haven't yet seen anyone doing the tending, but doubtless they have nipped in while we were out, or else will materialize in the near future.) One of the beds has a huge canna plant in, they remind me of candles, long thick stems with vivid orange flowers flaming from the top. Magic. There are geraniums, huge red geraniums. And roses of various colours, not a flower I would associate with Portugal, but then they do cultivate them in Africa, don't they, not a million miles away, I suppose.

    Anyway, the cacophony of colour is superb, and this little five minute feast for the eyes was a welcome treat before making the tea. I took it up to Henry and we lolled in bed, reading our books, chatting a little. Henry caressed my breasts, almost incidentally, as he read a junk novel he'd found downstairs.

    'F-funny old thing, isn't it,' he said, suddenly putting down his book and rolling over onto one elbow to gaze, somewhat disconcertingly, actually, into my eyes.

    'What is?'

    I had no idea at all what he was on about.

    'You know, sex,' he rejoindered, the circling of my nipple becoming somewhat more deliberate and attentive. There was a strange look in his eye, as if he was with me, yet far away. I took an executive decision, as I wanted to make the most of the day, not to become too embroiled in a deep discussion, particularly as my own sexual leanings had been somewhat titivated this last couple of weeks, and I didn't want to give anything away.

    'Funny, you think,' I said, and moved closer towards him, gently interrupting the incessant circling and taking his thigh between mine. I caressed his face. 'Okay, let's see how funny you think this is.'

I then proceeded to make love to him as quickly and as smartly as I knew how – me on top – so that we could still be at our destination by midday. I suppose that sounds a little calculated, but my molecules are still disturbed, and I didn't want to have to nurse him through any traumas if he sensed my straying mind. He seems to be making a very adequate recovery from his work addiction, and I really don't want complications. My seduction strategy didn't fully work, however. Once we were showered and dressed, had a light breakfast, let the maid in, and leaped into our lovely hire car – Citroen C3, perfectly adequate for two and surprisingly roomy – he began again.

'Do you think, Izzie, that you would ever seriously f-f-fancy anybody else?'

Shit. Henry's thought police have sussed the murky mind of his wife the infidel. How should I play it? I decided to be honest but general. That way I would be able to be true to myself while retaining an aspect of privacy. As you'll have gleaned, I believe that there's a great deal of difference between privacy and secrecy, and we're all entitled to a liberal dose of the former.

'Well, Henry,' I began, as a Portuguese driver raced up to my bumper with only centimetres to spare, forcing me to move swiftly into the inside lane, thus helping me to be in touch with the fragility of life. This clarified my sense of perspective about what's really important, and I was able to answer very truthfully and without shame.

'Well, yes, Henry,' I began. I could feel the earnest light of Henry's eyes boring into me, and glanced toward him. 'Hypothetically, of course. I mean, we fancy people all of the time, don't we?' Joe's rippling stomach came powerfully into mental view, and a thrill charged my groin. 'I mean, we're animals, aren't we? And if you were married to someone who never fancied anyone else – well, how dull would that be? It would mean that they weren't sexually alive.'

Henry was nodding, enthusiastically, it seemed to me. Encouraged, I went on.

'I mean, likewise if no one else ever flirted with your partner – I mean, who wants to be partnered by the only person in the world who nobody else finds attractive?'

'I suppose not.' Henry was with me all the way. 'I hadn't really thought of it like that. You're absolutely right.'

'But,' I expanded, (and this is where I might have begun to tangle myself up, given that I could have just left it there, but by now I was becoming fond of the sound of my own voice) 'if one is in a committed relationship to another, then of course you would draw the line at doing anything about fancying that other person. And then the fancying would just be a passing ember whose flames were never fanned.'

'I see,' said Henry. 'And do you think we can control whether or not we f-f-fan the f-f-f-f-flames?' I cringed; I couldn't have found a worse expression for Henry if I'd tried. Unless I'd been really witty and talked about fanning the fucking flames. Anyway, he managed to get the words out, so on we went. And to be honest I was intrigued. Poor lamb – he must be feeling very insecure.

'Absolutely, darling, absolutely.' I patted his thigh affectionately and looked his way. 'Of course we can. I mean, that's what separates us from the animals, isn't it?'

'I suppose you're right,' agreed Henry.

'Of course I'm right. Believe me, honey, a fancy is just a fancy – it really doesn't have to turn into anything else at all.' I risked a full head turn and a smile, then got swiftly back to keeping an eye on the traffic.

'I suppose you're right,' repeated dearly beloved, and he too risked a smile.

I hoped he felt better, and for a moment I felt guilty that I've disturbed his equilibrium so much. I mean, there he is, making the most generous and extravagant of birthday presents and there's me, having sexual fantasies about the pool man. So while I can't undertake not to have the fantasies, at the very least I could try and be more attentive to Henry.

Anyway, Henry must have heard what he'd needed to, because then he fiddled with the car radio and found Radio Kiss, an English channel and soon we were singing along to 'Spirit in the Sky', and 'I Want to Know What Love Is', and exchanging conspiratorial eye contact, until we came to the turn off the motorway that I was waiting for. Henry was intrigued.

'Hmm, Albufeira and Guia,' he noticed. 'So where could we be going? Aha!' he exclaimed, 'we're going to Algarve Shopping!'

I smiled inwardly. Dear old Henry, miles off: brilliant that he hadn't guessed yet.

'No, try again,' I said, but he couldn't get it and so looked totally surprised when we pulled into the entrance of Zoomarine.

'Oh my God,' said Henry, looking woefully up to the Ferris wheel which towered over the entrance scene, 'we're going to see the dolphins.'

'Absolutely,' I crowed, 'and we're going to see if you want to swim with them.'

Henry looked alarmed.

'We'll watch the show at any rate,' I said, 'and then decide if we want to book in for another time. Perhaps when the others are here?'

He heaved what sounded like a sigh of relief. Henry would like to be adventurous, but in fact is naturally cautious – a wimp by any other name – so I knew already that it might be too much if we just came to swim 'cold' as it were. And to be honest, I knew that, like me, he has very mixed feelings about animals in captivity. I mean to say, yes, it's great that we can see them, but they can be somewhat cramped, away from their natural habitat. I remember taking Connie and Jon to Dudley Zoo years ago and seeing two chimps fornicating in what looked like a most unprepossessing scene bordering on rape. I hadn't been back to a zoo since.

As it happened, we turned out to have an awesome few hours, and if there were some mixed moments, they were not on account of the dolphins. We began with an exhibition of fancy birds – parrots, parakeets, all sorts – which pedalled balls across a table, came back to their owners, and so on. They were very well trained, and very clever. Then we wandered around and went up on the Ferris wheel which turned slowly, enabling us to have a terrific view of the Algarve. Then lunch (that early morning sex certainly gives you an appetite☺), at a hot chicken café which took forever but which served the most succulent chicken, as ever in the Algarve.

The next show was the sea lions, in a new production of Peter Pan. They were well trained, and splashed about and waddled at all the right parts, but were very much performing seals, so to speak. Then we saw the hunting birds, falcons, owls, of all sizes and descriptions. The birds swooped over the audiences heads, magnificent in their flight.

'Just like paragliding,' teased Henry, looking rapt. I was so pleased.

Then we went on to try some other rides, although Henry drew the line at the swing boat.

'No,' he said, looking quite pale, 'they always make me want to stand up. I went from school with my year, and everyone started to tease me f-for being s-scared, and then gravity just made me stand right up and I f-f-fell f-f-flat on my f-f-f'' – here I was longing to say the word for him, but I know he hates that, so I waited for 'face' and then made it clear that it really was of no significance whether we went on the swing boat or not.

So by the time we got to see the dolphins, we'd had quite some fun and were ready for the main treat of the day.

And what a treat.

The dolphins whooshed through to the huge pool, taking my breath away, leaping in formations, diving in formation, huge and elegant. They're amazing. The trainers introduced each dolphin to us, and then they performed turn after turn in perfect synchronicity, the trainers riding their backs, and constantly rewarding them with fish. I was moved to tears by the intelligence before me and also by the obviously brilliant relationship that the trainers and dolphins had together.

Henry was also wowed, and as we left he decided that it might be nice to swim with them, and that he would broach it with the friends and family. It might be an attractive activity for after the party, a kind of special and intimate event. Rosie would love it, I'm sure, although Connie might be a bit stuffy. We'll have to see.

Anyway, Henry gave me a huge hug in the car park as we left, and said what a lovely day he'd had. We drove back to our villa and then walked down the road for a very simple meal of soup and salad. We had a drink in the Rainbow bar afterwards, and I noticed as we left that Joe and Vlad were sitting on one of the other tables. I didn't know whether to wave or not, as my stomach had lurched somewhat when I caught Joe's eye, but Henry took away any cause for concern by waving very cheerily and indeed going over to shake hands with both men. Who invited us to stay for a beer. Henry said he'd love to but had to get home to check his e-mails, so maybe later? I said no at this point, as after today's conversation I didn't want to give myself away, and even if I misbehave in future, this was Henry's day, so it seemed only noble to dedicate myself to him.

So they were a success, those old dolphins, and I must say that I'm looking forward to going again and maybe even getting in the pool. *And* I'm looking forward to tomorrow, when life as we know it at the villa will change with the arrival of my lovely old friends. I can't wait to see them, and I just know that we're going to have the best time.

I shall make us a night cap now I think, perhaps a decaffeinated coffee with a shot or two of brandy, and then see if I can't get Henry away from his e-mails and off to bed. With our books. Like the cosy old couple that we have become. And I shall take my own advice, which has been ringing in my ears all day long.

Just because I fancy someone with a vengeance does not mean I have to fan the flames.

first arrivals

april 13th 2010

It's a lovely day today. The sun is already hot, and I have had my early morning swim – seventy lengths today, forty breast, ten legs only while holding on to my rubber ring, ten crawl and ten backstroke. An effortlessly even distribution of toning and anaerobic exercise. Looking in the mirror, I reckon the self-discipline and simple holiday regime is paying off. The fat on my bottom is definitely smoother, and my shorts are just a wee bit looser than usual.

I'm going to collect both Jutta and Tammi. They've met each other a few times, just at occasional functions or on girly nights, and I'm sure they'll be fine. Tammi is a book editor, she's sharp to the point of injury, but she's well meaning enough. Being a counsellor, Jutta will be non-judgmental of Tammi and supportive to her.

I know they'll be fine.

I've decided to drive to Faro myself, it's more or less just one road, the A22, and I'm quite confident I can manage to stay on the right side of the road, especially after going as far as Zoomarine yesterday. Henry has offered to come with me, but to be honest, I shall welcome the space, so I told him that the girls will have far too much luggage for that to be possible. I can't wait to see them both, and tonight I've booked a table at *O Porco*, the poshest restaurant in the village.

Joe is here – again – with Vlad. I'm assuming Vlad's Russian, but he could be Ukrainian I suppose. How does one know these things? You can tell the English abroad, though, can't you, something about their propensity to go out without their hair done properly, the cut of their shorts, and the certain knowledge that they have saved up and planned out carefully that awful semi-lycra outfit that should have stayed right there in Matalan, bargain or no bargain, where it belonged.

Anyway, Joe and I have had a bit of the old frisson going, so I'm glad I've got my super serum on today. I gave him and Vlad a beer each. Actually, Vlad did the pool more or less on his own, while Joe talked to me. He wanted to know what I did for a living. When I told him I teach adults, he seemed really interested. He kind of looked me up and down in that non-eye movement way again and said,

'I bet you could teach me a thing or two.'

Must confess I found it alarmingly easy to offer a fairly saucy rejoinder.

'I'm sure I could. What areas of your education do you think you need particular help with?' I was drinking a smoothie, as it's zero tolerance on the roads. I took a sip, in what I hoped was a sexy kind of way. I could feel the erotic charge between us. When the smoothie frothed over, though, and spilled down my lips I did suddenly feel really silly and could see Henry and Vlad looking at me across the pool. Henry was keeping Vlad entertained, which I thought was kind really, and was having a glass of red wine to match Vlad's beer.

I laughed in what I intended to be a relatively coquettish-yet-mature way, and put my drink down, giving myself a metaphorical shake. I was definitely flame-fanning, and needed to stop, as I was being as subtle as a pair of bellows.

'I have to go to the airport,' I said, 'two of my very good friends are coming to stay.'

'Okay,' said Joe, 'well, we'll probably be in the Praia bar later on if you guys are going out.'

I stored this information, smiled, and made my exit. Then I dressed, loose trousers and a red shirt, and can see that my tan looks well against this outfit. I left Henry in the bedroom looking out over the pool, and apparently agonising what to wear tonight, of all things. I fear it will be the fawn slacks that I've worked so hard to discourage him from, but never mind. I've just nipped on here to check the flight times, couldn't resist a little update, and now I'm off.

Sooo excited.

*

I got to the airport a little early, after a lovely drive up the A22, the mountains of Monchique on my left and the sea on my right, with all the cares I might imagine I had just falling off my shoulders. I put on a playlist that I'd made for one of our rare parties once, a New Year's one I think, and sang along to Annie Lennox, *Runaway from You*, and Chrissie Hynds, *Stop Your Sobbing*, and of course Janis, and Aretha, all those fab Diva women of my generation. I felt quite hoarse yet refreshed when I pulled into the car park, and walked confidently up to arrivals. The plane was slightly earlier than it had said (or I was longer on the laptop☺) so my friends were through baggage collection and I saw them immediately.

How would I not? Jutta, tall and slim with pale red hair, wearing a bright blue duffle coat of all things, and long faded jeans, Tammi neat and short, in a smart and well thought out casual suit, very short dark hair spiked with gel, and boots whose heels could kill if she were ever inclined to embed them in someone's head.

They both looked tense, standing a little way away from each other. My heart missed a beat. I hoped that Jutta hadn't been too counselly, prying into Tammi's sexual issues again. She's well meaning, but can be a bit overbearing. I waved at them until Jutta glanced up and saw me – woohoo! Jutta walked quickly towards me, and within seconds was holding me in one of her infamous bear hugs. Tammi followed up, kissing me in more reserved fashion, once on each cheek, then looking at me in her compulsively flirtatious style.

'Wow, am I ever glad to get off a plane,' she said, sideways daggers emanating from her green eyes and spearing Jutta from six paces.

'Yes, it was a bit intense, all that stuff about your girlfriend,' said Jutta, 'but I really do think that you need to resolve those issues you know.'

Tammi stopped dead, causing the person behind her to emergency stop his luggage trolley, jettisoning two duty free bags from the hand luggage section. Tammi never flinched, didn't hear the clang of liquor bottles on the cold tiled floor. She took a deep breath.

'Look, Jutta, are you or are you not my sexual adviser?'

The wronged man looked up from the floor, where he was chasing the bottles, with interest, while his wife tried to usher their two small children away.

'Well no, Tammi, but I have done a lot of relationship and sexual counselling.' Jutta sounded perplexed.

'I said, Jutta, are you or are you not my sexual adviser?'

I could see Jutta taking a calming breath as she answered.

'No, Tammi, I'm not.'

'Well good. Maybe you'll have the decency to stay out of my hair then, because if I ever want your *fucking* advice, I'll ask for it.'

The man stood up, his bottles gathered, looking impressed. I smiled at him and then made it my business to get Jutta and Tammi out of there as quickly as possible. It seemed that the flight had not gone as smoothly as I'd hoped.

'Come on you two, I've just got to pay my parking ticket.'

As soon as we walked outside the terminal, I could see the balmy air working instant magic on both my friends, and Jutta smiled a big sorry at Tammi, then went on to exclaim on the blueness of the sky and the heat of the sun, the waving of the palm trees, and once we were in the car, they both began to unwind, on the surface at least. I knew Tammi would have to bend my ear later, to work through whatever rage had been provoked in her, and I knew that Jutta would need support as whatever she'd said, I knew it would be from her compulsion to help people, even those that didn't need it, often those who needed it but didn't want it. Jutta's enthusiasm frequently meant that she sometimes saw problems where there weren't any before she made her well intentioned interventions.

We put the luggage in the boot, piled in the car and caught up with preliminaries on the way to the villa. Yes, I was having a nice time. Henry was fine. Jutta's general take on Henry is that he is too tense, not assertive enough, and not big enough on self-determination. Tammi gets on with him really well: they can talk about anything, and flirt with each other in the real sense of the word, knowing it will never lead anywhere. Tammi likes his soft side, his lack of machismo; she was looking forward to seeing him.

Jutta told me she's changed jobs, diversifying to include a bit of executive coaching among the counselling. She's also working in a project for the homeless, many of whom have problems of dependency.

'And of course, they often have problems in how to relate to people.'

'So are you in a relationship, then Jutta? Must be interesting to be such an expert.' Ouch, Tammi was not playing nice. I felt protective of Jutta. Despite all the soul searching, the expertise on how people relate to each other, Jutta finds actually doing it very difficult, which clearly Tammi knows.

'No, I'm single just now.' Jutta took another calming breath. 'And of course we already know about yours, you told me on the plane.'

Dear Tammi, she had no problem in pulling at all, gorgeous looks, fab personality, and so clever. I turned to her.

'Yes, what's happening with Jamie?'

'We split up, two weeks ago.'

'Never! Why, what happened?' Tammi's relationships always fascinate me, she takes such risks, which I have to say I've always admired her for. And she's unconventional, very much her own woman. I suppose if I'm honest I sometimes get a thrill from listening to her adventures.

I would never disclose this to Jutta, as her analysis of my vicarious pleasures would be far too difficult to listen to.

'Well, Jamie's job was very demanding. And then there was the PhD. It was like we never got time to see each other much, kind of stagnated a bit.'

Knowing Tammi so well, I suspect there is someone else on the scene, 'the catalyst' as she always dubs the new lover. Never being one to be pushy, I thought it better to wait until she wants to talk to me on our own.

'Aah,' I said.

'Aah, the stage of norming, just can go on a bit long.' Jutta nodded sagely. I caught Tammi's eye in the mirror, and she winked at me.

I must have been more distracted than I thought, because suddenly Jutta was shouting 'Watch that car!', and I brought my attention right back to the vehicle that had appeared from nowhere and was overtaking me. I was so relaxed and at home with my old friends, I was driving like I was back in England, which was not so clever, not when it involved veering to the wrong side of the road. The roads are treacherous enough without this scatty dimension. Portuguese drivers seem to want to get in your boot, then suddenly a whole fleet appear from nowhere to overtake you, frightening you half to death.

I concentrated on driving.

When we got back to the villa, I noticed that Henry looked quite flushed and animated. He'd prepared us all a lovely brunch, fresh bread and croissants, cheeses, sausages, olives, jams and honey, and opened wine for us, even though the sun was barely past the midday dial. He and Tammi embraced.

'Lots to tell you,' she confided excitedly.

'You too,' he said, before kissing Jutta twice, once on each cheek. I was proud of him: he seems to be getting really quite Portuguese.

We found it hard deciding who should have which room, because although both have a double bed, only one has an ensuite bathroom, and we don't want one of them to feel more favoured than the other. In the end, I suggested that Jutta should have the ensuite, as she isn't used to sharing at all, and can be private if by chance she scores☺.

While Tammi will be okay sharing a bathroom with Atilla, when she arrives.

Or if she arrives. I haven't spoken to her since I've been here, which I must address.

The rest of the family will be staying next door, as I don't want anybody to feel cramped, which coincidentally suits me as I am just a tad unsure as to how it will be to have my whole family under one roof for a whole week: not that I would let that little selfish gene get in the way, but it is nice to have a real reason why that isn't possible. And it's great that Tammi and Jutta are here for a few days first, giving them legitimate first claim on the house.

Anyway, once unpacked, we tucked into a few tasty morsels and sampled the wine. Henry has pushed the boat out, this was one of the finer Dão wines, at least six euros a bottle, and he'd also got some Casal Garcia on ice. Everyone relaxed as the deep red and light nectars respectively washed down the delicious bread rolls, and it wasn't long before Jutta and Tammi were getting along fine.

'Lovely pool,' said Jutta, and soon moved herself to a sunbed, its back upright, and encouraged us all to do the same. 'I feel resplendently replete.'

We giggled at her alluring alliteration.

Henry joined in. 'The pool is our perfectly positive p-pleasure.' He beamed: we smiled. 'The pool is a bit of a l-luxury. Pool men are very good. Seem to be coming twice or three times a week now.'

I swear he glanced at me quizzically, and I tried very hard not to blush, although to be honest, I was probably as pink as Henry already, given the sun and the wine.

'Yes,' I said brazenly, 'absolutely gorgeous.'

I don't know, I sometimes wish that Henry would be a little bit more on the ball, just a tad jealous perhaps, or threateningly flirtatious with my friends, instead of which he tolerates anything I say or do. So on this occasion, as usual, he just smiled fondly at me and then turned his attention to Tammi.

'So, what's happening in good old blighty then, Tam?'

He nudged her foot affectionately with his.

'Nothing good,' she rejoindered, 'it's all bloody all over the place. I've got six Issue sellers within a stone's throw, everybody's house value has gone down, which is good for some I suppose. I have to pay a fortune just to get into my own city centre because of this city centre tax lark. And now we've got Tweedle Cam and Tweedle Clegg, touting their policies to the highest bidder like a pair of old tarts. And the troops abroad have not only made it easier for the heroin trade worldwide, but even the bloody Afghans' addiction rates have doubled so they can escape the misery of their slave labour, making carpets for all our bloody homes. Price of petrol's through the roof, and half of England is verging on fascism as the media whips up fear about immigrants. Honestly, Henry, don't you ever just think it's one great big bloody trap that they've got us all in while they screw oil out of Iraq and then secretly sell it to the Chinese?'

And that was that. The afternoon went with a bang. We put the world to rights, argued over whether or not there should be more 'social' housing, swapped horror stories about the NHS, shared our views about education, drank more wine, and then dived in for the inevitable drunken swim. We had a whale of a time, and it was some time later that I realised I'd forgotten to top up my factor 50 face protection. I've had to use lashings of aftersun cream and pray to God that my lips don't blister.

We're all showered now, ready to head to the restaurant. I understand that they garnish their food with lots of fruit, so I'll have to nab what slices of cucumber I can and pat them around my essential bits.

I've scrubbed up well, even though I do say so myself. These low waisted fashions suit me (actually, with hipsters and flares, I'm in my element, and although I know I'm not seventeen again, I think I'd get away for a young thirties tonight, especially if the light is right). I'm looking forward to the meal. We might just go to the Praia bar afterwards for a drink.

For the girls, of course, they would love to sit out under the stars drinking pina colada, the sound of the waves crashing within yards of us.

So I think that's what we'll do.

Tchau for now x

pause for thought

april 14th 2010

Well, thank goodness for cucumber eye pads. I woke very early and those little bags under my eyes were crammed full with white wine, champagne, and pina coladas. What a night! At the end of it I felt sure I'd sleep for hours, but no, I woke up really early, heart pounding and body glowing in the bed. I've dampened my forehead and taken a spoonful of agnus castus.

Perhaps writing the events of the evening will calm me.

We had the most amazing meal down in the village. Henry had those lovely garlic prawns which I adore, but they can be so messy to eat and it's all too easy to splash the garlicky oil down one's trousers, so I settled for letting him peel me one and pass it carefully across the table. Meanwhile, I indulged in melon with Parma ham, a whole half melon, exquisitely cut and just perfectly ripe. Jutta went for good old Portuguese *sopa de legumes*, which is so much better than vegetable soup at home, and Tammi went for *marisco*.

Well, you should have seen her plate, just everything – prawns, oysters, clams, pieces of monkfish, squid, and every dish so well garnished with *fruta da terra* – Tammi got quite rude when she started on the figs, which Henry seemed to find amusing.

Then we all had steaks, which caused Jutta some problems at first because she was trying to stay vegetarian – nothing with a face, as she coins it. I assured her that the cattle round here are home procured and fed on the most luscious organic food, which I think they must be because the steaks *are* particularly gorgeous, so she went for it. We ordered four peppered steaks, and oodles of fresh vegetables, which made it okay because between that and the cattle's diet, we were being virtually vegetarian by default!

We talked about all sorts of things. First, Tammi's break up with Jamie. I got her to admit that there was someone else, Annie, a woman who works in her company. This is causing Tammi some problems because she always makes it a rule not to blur the boundaries of business and pleasure. Then, inevitably, the whole sexuality conversation, which of course Jutta started: is sexual preference genetically determined or socially constructed, which we all have strong views on. Jutta was being just a little bit conservative I thought, but then that's Jutta for you, all that unconditional positive regard to throw around but some very tightly wrapped views. Whereas Henry was being most liberal, very supportive to Tammi, and put some really interesting points, including the view that people might change over the course of a lifetime, and concluding that it didn't really matter how sexual preference is determined, everyone has the right to their preferences, and it's about time society got over it. Well done Henry, I say, and that gave Tammi a bit of cue to change the subject completely to her work, giving us the low-down on different authors, hearing what the latest book prizes are saying about literature, and so on. I wanted to know how people got on to book judging panels. How, for example, did that slimy article Michael Portillo get to judge the Man Booker prize? I still remember the country cheering when he lost his seat at the 1997 elections, and now he's some kind of celebrity critic. And that of course led us back to the sexuality question, as it seems that since he's come out, everyone's forgiven the fact that he was so right-wing and abhorrent.

And so on.

Anyway, suffice to say that we were a heady mix of wit, culture and bonhomie by the time we left our table, and there was full agreement to carry on with another bottle of wine and some pina coladas in the Praia bar. I went and checked my makeup, which I'd applied carefully to look natural, just in case a certain someone was to turn up in Praia bar: older women look so awful with black eyeliner and deep red lipstick.

I was really enjoying Henry, though, thinking how lucky I was to have him, so I don't know what I was doing even thinking of Joe.

But I was.

The Praia bar is a concrete and wooden construction, at the bottom of the hill that takes you down to the sea, which it faces. So you have to climb up some steps to get to it, and then you can sit outside and see the moonlight on the sea, and hear the lap of the water – quite special. It was fairly empty at first. I guess we'd been typically English in eating at 7.30 rather than later, but then these days we do have digestion to consider. It doesn't do to go to bed on a full stomach, Attila always says, and somewhat grudgingly I must say that I've begun to agree with her. Anyway, this meant that we were in the bar before ten o'clock.

We continued our conversations and I tried to be relaxed, though I did find myself looking over my shoulder now and again, until eventually Joe and Vlad came in with a couple of other guys, and blow me, they came over and took the table right next to ours.

We exchanged hellos and Henry and I introduced our guests to the lads, and they introduced their two friends so the formalities were done and everyone carried on chatting.

It's slightly hazy after that, the haze illuminated by some choice specific images which shine through with alarming clarity. We didn't so much talk with the lads to begin with as much as exchange a few asides, but I know that Joe winked at me once or twice, and Vlad looked at our table with a slightly hungry look in his eyes, towards Jutta. She could do with a nice romantic interlude.

But then we were rudely interrupted by a fairly drunken German man.

Helmut (as it turned out he couldn't be more aptly named, but you'll see why in a minute) was what I used to call middle-aged but now realise is fairly young, maybe late forties. He had a beard and moustache. He asked first of all where we were staying, all that sort of thing, said where he was staying, how he liked golf, and was just slightly creepy in the way he was looking at us. At some point during this episode, Henry had turned his chair to chat to Joe and Vlad about the possibility of freshwater fishing being introduced to Portugal. So Helmut had kind of squeezed himself in between us girls. He was looking quite lecherous, most unattractive, and inevitably asked us all what we did. Tammi by then was in her element, pissed off but dry with it. She answered him with a smile on her face.

'I'm a mud wrestler,' she said sweetly, 'my name is Ruby.' She turned to Jutta. 'This is my friend Pearl, she works at Zoomarine with the dolphins.' Jutta smiled sweetly.

'Guten Abend,' she said.

'And this,' Tammi went on, indicating my good self, 'is Emerald. She's a high class call girl who's taken early retirement.' I giggled despite myself, and noticed now that we had the attention of the lads. Joe's eyebrow shot up with a knowing smile, and I flushed. The German hesitated.

'No, you are having me on.'

'On the contrary,' Tammi purred, 'I would say that I'd show you my muscles to prove it. But I only perform for women.' She sipped pina colada through her straw. Helmut broke into a grin.

'Ah, I see what you are doing. You are trying to take the mickey out of me.' He chuckled.

'No, not at all. Just answering your questions.'

Henry and Vlad continued to discuss the finer points of fly fishing versus pole fishing.

'Okay.' Helmut grinned. 'I was just trying to be friendly. But now I see that you want to play games with me. Okay, I can play your game. I tell you, my friends, I am not out to "pull you", I am not pretending that I am the man with the very big dick that is the answer to your dreams. On the contrary, I have a very small dick, it is like this.'

He waggled his little finger in the air, and we laughed, despite the unseemliness of his behaviour.

But then he really went too far.

'And to prove to you, I will take out my dick now and show you.' We looked at each other agape: surely not. Tammi was annoyed and all set to help him embarrass himself.

'Go on then, Helmut,' she said. 'Show us your helmet.'

And to our horror, Helmut duly unzipped his grey casuals and began to unleash his penis in front of our very eyes.

'Oi.' The next thing I knew Joe and the bartender had hold of Helmut, one either side, and Tammi just managed to get in a 'Oh yes, you were right, it is a tiny little thing,' as Helmut was encouraged to leave the bar in three large steps, his feet hardly touching the ground, and his jacket following. Henry looked up, bewildered, and for a moment no one knew what to do, but of course we ended up collapsing in laughter. It was clear that the bartender wasn't going to ask us to leave; *au contraire*, he sent over a new tray of pina coladas by way of apology, and then the ice was well and truly broken, and our tables were pushed together. Joe sat next to me while everyone seemed to be engaged in lively conversation: our thighs brushed from time to time, and my heart raced.

I do hope that I didn't make a complete fool of myself. I found out quite a lot about Joe – bright young man, dropped out of college as he 'needed some space,' but intends to go back at some time and complete his degree in philosophy and politics.

Fascinating. He seemed really interested in my compulsion to English Literature, declared admiration for Sebastian Faulks, one of my favourite authors, and seemed to be a good conversationalist all round.

I think I might have told him too much about my family, although he was kind enough to say that I didn't look old enough to have a daughter Constantine's age. He also said how much he liked the more mature women, so much more interesting than young skinny things, and I remember thinking how refreshing, a young man with insight. Jutta leaned over at some point and whispered 'classic Oedipal complex', to which I think I might have told her to 'fuck off and lighten up' before encouraging her to go and talk to Vlad.

Eventually, seamlessly it seemed, we ended up dancing on the verandah. Joe danced with Tammi, which I thought was sweet and clever, while Henry danced with me. Right behind him, his back to Henry's back, Vlad was dancing with Jutta. I was thrilled. All kinds of good things could come out of this birthday month, and here I was amongst my best friends, with my lover, and even managing to enjoy a flattering flirtation. Zen moment or what.

So we were strutting to *Simply the Best*, and I was thinking how fab that the Portuguese accommodate the English so well (and the Eastern Europeans – really cosmopolitan), when Jutta strutted a strut too far, right down the top three concrete steps of the bar. She landed awkwardly, her long gypsy skirt riding up to her waist, her legs parting in unseemly fashion, so that her backside was on full view. And although thongs *can* be very sexy, the sight of Jutta's white exposed and dimpled buttocks was not perhaps as erotic as she might have hoped. Maybe they're best left to the younger woman after all. They don't seem to have much gusset to them, do they, and I think you need a bit of a gusset at our age. Now that makes sense of why my grandmother actually used to darn gussets, a little domestic skill which is long gone from the female repertoire.

Anyway, I think those little boxer shapes for me from now on.

I digress. We picked Jutta up as quickly as possible, and the lads rallied round and helped to carry her home in a fireman's cradle, Tammi and I singing *Swing Low, Sweet Chariot*, turning our faces and hands to the beautiful stars, and generally feeling very spiritual and at one with the world. Once home, we packed the ankle with ice until the swelling subsided. I'm afraid that Jutta cried, which left mascara and bloatedness all round her eyes, but Vlad was still attentive enough to kiss her tenderly on both cheeks before he went. Indeed he went on to kiss us all, including Henry, which I thought quaint. I wonder if that's a Russian thing? Joe only kissed the women, and I just hope that he felt as I did when his lips brushed both my cheeks, for I swear his touch on my face was like a torch to brushwood, igniting the fires within to an almost unbearable heat.

We got Jutta to bed, and Tammi, Henry and I had a medicinal brandy. Henry was most responsive when I initiated a silent sexual interlude with him, trying not to groan too loudly or to move too many bedsprings, and he seemed highly aroused too.

Perhaps it had been the sight of Jutta's bottom☺.

I hope that Jutta's swelling has gone down. Vlad was very concerned and said that he would like to come and enquire after her, if that would be okay with us, so I wonder if he'll keep his word? I wouldn't like to see her let down in love again.

shopping in Lagos

april 15th 2010

Well, everyone was not too bad when they all eventually got up yesterday morning, Henry looked happy, a little smile playing around his lips, and why not when he's with some of his favourite people. He does love my women friends, especially Tammi, as I said, and is really glad they're here. He's a bit in dread of all the children and Attila arriving in one batch, for which I can't blame him, as to be honest, I'm bloody terrified. Jutta was in surprisingly good form. Her ankle was a bit bruised looking, but nothing like as bad as we thought, and she had quite a glow to her face.

Tammi didn't surface until nearly midday, then it was straight into the pool before a light breakfast. Her body is still in really good shape. Tammi has always been one for the gym, and it's no shilly-shallying for her when she's in the pool either. She must have swam at a pace for at least twenty minutes, no floating around, lots of calories to keep active in her lithe body. She caught me looking at her long lean legs and gave me one of her come-on smiles. She knows though, Tammi, where I'm at, and accepts my sexual preferences with no need to challenge me, as I do hers, so we're safe to flirt.

Henry was a darling. He made sure there was enough shopping in for there to be something for everyone. He sang around the place, and all the unpleasant trappings of work seem to be well behind him now, to the point where he has his Blackberry switched off virtually all the time.

'From now on, d-darling, I'm only going to check messages at lunchtime and coffee breaks,' he boasted. I notice also that he hasn't been stuttering quite so much, always a sign that he's relaxing.

Stutters are weird, aren't they, I think they still don't fully understand the cause of a stutter. Henry once told me about how his parents tried to get him out of stuttering when he was a child. Henry said it was to be helpful but my cynical side, I'm afraid, tends to believe that they were furious because he wasn't perfect. There he was, f-f-f-flawed, no getting away from it. Couldn't even have a speech impediment that sound posh or fey, like a lisp or

106

something. Just a plain old stutter. What a letdown for James and Mildred.

I asked him what they'd done.

'Child Guidance Clinic every week for a year. I had to read out loud in time to a metronome, can you imagine? I learned how to give every syll-a-ble-the-same-em-pha-sis. No use to me at all. Everyone would only make f-f-fun of me if I tried that at home.'

He'd laughed at himself when he told me. Then, apparently, a trainee clinical psychologist had a go at him with some medication. He reckoned this made no difference, and as he was now seventeen, and the trainee psychologist only twenty-two, and they began to see each other at the same parties, Henry refused to continue treatment.

Personally, I think James and Mildred should just have accepted him as he is, warts and all, and taken a bit more notice of how scared he was of them, and how he doesn't stutter when he's angry. As he gets older it's not such a problem, more a delightful idiosyncrasy, and it's great to note it virtually disappearing. And when he's had a few drinks, well, there's hardly a hesitation at all.

So, yesterday slipped past in a down time warp, and today we spent the day chilling out until late afternoon when we went into Lagos to shop. Shopping is a leveller; everyone can do it. Tammi bought one or two lovely pieces for her apartment from a gorgeous African type shop, pricey I thought, but nice, while Jutta was keen on finding a different dress for my party. Vlad's attentions have clearly perked her up. And Henry, to my delight, indulged in a silk paisley shirt, so unlike his usual starchy style. I bought a silver bracelet with large gaudy stones in, avant-garde and irresistible. I had a second's wonder whether it's too young for me, but I can always pass it on to Rosie.

I'm looking forward to seeing Rosie. She comes the day after tomorrow, the first of the family to arrive. I shall like that.

Anyway, then we went on to a fab Indian restaurant. Well, truth be told, we stopped off at a cocktail bar first. I had another Pina Colada, while Tammi went for Sex on the Beach followed by a Shady Lady, and Jutta stuck to Screwdrivers – and Henry, egged on by Tammi, naughty girl, had two Hard Dicks, a concoction of vodka, soda and frangelico. So we were quite merry by the time we got to the restaurant, where the food was supreme. We washed it down with a beer, not our usual, but when in Rome and so on, so we had pints of Cobra all round. We rolled back to the villa in a taxi, and then blow me if Henry didn't fancy a little walk down to the village bar. We were quite late and there was nobody about. We were all a tiny bit disappointed, but personally I was most disappointed for Jutta, as it would have been nice if Vlad was there.

We've all drunk herbal tea back at home in a lame effort to detox before bedtime. I'm a bit restless, so thought I'd do my writing catch up. I can hear Jutta playing low beat music upstairs. Henry's playing with the guitar which was stored on a stand in the back bedroom. I'm enjoying a quiet Dunhill menthol with another herbal tea, this one for 'calming and revitalising', and I'm also running a bath. I shall go soon and have a deep soak, while applying a face mask, both for relaxation and for skin rejuvenation, and I'm sure it will be wonderful.

And then, with luck and somewhat disloyally, I shall dream of Joe, whose erection I can imagine at the drop of a hat. And Henry, my dear insecure Henry will neither know nor care about my unfanned fantasies.

a surge of heat

april 16th 2010

Hoorah for Henry! This morning he brought me breakfast in bed, on a tray. Juice freshly squeezed out of oranges taken from the tree next door, bread rolls still slightly warm from the *padaria*, butter and marmalade, and *café com leite*. A jamboree of colour and flavour.

I ate with real enjoyment, and felt positively spoilt. Henry said something about a couple of things he needed to check in to the office about, but first, unusually, he got down to the floor and did fifty press-ups and fifty sit-ups.

'Use it, don't lose it,' he remarked cheerfully.

I was impressed, and it certainly made for good entertainment while I ate. I noticed also that he has clipped his nose hairs, not something he does every day.

What a sweetheart.

I felt like doing nothing at all today. It won't surprise you to know that I dreamt of *him* last night, and I also had a vague awareness of Henry being rather frisky through his boxer shorts. When Henry went to shower, I got out of bed and opened the double doors onto the verandah. The only thing that could make this lovely villa any better would be if we could see the sea, but it's nice knowing that it's only just over the horizon and I can smell it in the air. Water is full of negative ions or some such thing: whatever it is, it's certainly doing me the world of good. So far, on almost every day the sky has been a deep turquoise, and the light is iridescent. For anyone who is artistically inclined, this is paradise.

Actually, it's paradise for us all.

While I was on the verandah, I heard the tinkling of bells. First it was a gentle sound, distant and ethereal, then it got stronger, a whole orchestra of bells, slightly different tones and volumes. I looked down the road to the bend, as I heard it coming nearer, gathering force, blending with the sounds of lowing and bleating, and suddenly, there came a herd of goats. Just yards away, in the middle of the road. Fascinating creatures close up – nanny goats with great big beards (and I think I've got problems!), Billy goats with great horns, and some that I took to be kids. There were brown ones, grey ones, black ones, mixed ones. And there, right in the middle, the goatherd. Tall, thirtyish, bronzed, dark-eyed, longish black hair. Trousers tucked into sturdy boots, dark waistcoat over a glistening firm torso, and bag slung casually across his body. And, a large, long walking stick.

What a treat.

I mean, you don't see goats like that every day at home.

I enjoyed the view until I heard Henry come out of the shower downstairs, went into the ensuite (which has kind of become mine – his and her bathrooms, very swish) – and body brushed, and took a short and refreshing shower myself. I had a great exfoliate with my apricot oil scrub, and felt much better for knowing that all those dead skin cells were off my premises. I perused self in the mirror, and noticed that my tummy is really quite brown. And actually, not in bad shape at all. I don't suppose there's time to diet before my party – it's on Saturday, not a million miles away now – but there are times, I can tell you, when I rue the passing of the Energen roll.

Anyway, then I too did some exercising, courtesy of dear old Pilates band. Henry came back in just as I was bending down doing my final stretch.

'Nice arse, honey,' he said, an expression I don't usually associate with Henry. I received the compliment with grace, nonetheless. He had brought up another tray of coffee, which we sat and drank at the little terrace table on the verandah.

'Do you think,' said Henry, as if from nowhere, 'do you think that we are all, at heart, bisexual?' I have to say that the question took me by surprise. You can tell that Tammi is having her impact. She's so totally at ease with herself in every way that the topic of sexuality often work its way into the agendas when she's present.

Maybe Henry is fancying her, and wondering whether he is the man to turn her, hoping that she really is bisexual after all? Maybe he thinks I fancy her?

This on top of the conversation we had on the way to Zoomarine.

'I think we probably are, deep down,' I said, and squeezed his arm reassuringly. 'But don't worry, I've made my choice and I'm not going to go gay on you now.'

With that I leaned over and gave him a big kiss.

110

'Though Tammi really is gay, you know,' I threw in for good measure. He looked at me a little quizzically, but I think he felt better for the touch of reassurance.

The irony of the situation didn't escape me, as I tucked my heterosexual fantasies deeper down into my psyche.

I decided to spend the whole day at the villa, eating little, swimming a lot and topping up my tan. I took a sunlounger at around ten thirty, and smothered myself in factor 25, with factor 50 on my face and a hat on my head. I was reading a book by Zoe Fairbairns, which curiously enough was about a woman of a certain age who became besotted with a man thirty years her junior.

Interesting.

As it happened, I was alone for the first half hour. It seemed that Tammi had arisen quite early, had her swim and gone walking. Jutta was laid up in her room resting her ankle, and Henry had taken her coffee and croissants, bless. So I soaked up some rays and then swam a casual fifty lengths, a little speed here and there to get the old heart rate up, and the usual twenty lengths legs only. My backside is definitely firmer, if I say so myself – and clearly Henry appreciated it this morning.

The next thing I knew I must have dozed off, for when I opened my eyes I was carefully shaded by a sun umbrella, courtesy of my dear husband, and he seemed to be setting the table for lunch.

'What time is it?' I asked, and Henry told me that it was 12.30 and that lunch would be served at one.

'And we have guests,' he said.

'I know we do. Where are they?'

'No, not those guests. Tammi's just gone to change, and Jutta's showering. No. I bumped into Joe in the village, at the *padaria* this morning. He said it was our day for the pool, so I said why don't they come and have a couple of beers and a spot of lunch.'

He looked at me for confirmation that this was a good idea. Naturally, I thought it was a great idea, yet I was also suspicious. Given all Henry's questions of late on matters sexual, I do wonder if he's testing me out in some way. So I tried not to be too enthusiastic.

'Whatever you think, darling,' I said, and waited a few minutes before casually going upstairs and finding a long light cream shirt to wear over my bikini, and applying a little light make-up and a touch of Chanel. No. 5. When I came out, there was Jutta, positioned carefully at the table with one leg up on a footstool, and looking radiant.

'Hey honey,' she said, as I stooped to give her a big hug. 'I've had such a slothful morning. It's been fabulous. I really feel like I'm making time for me just now, cherishing my inner child *and* rejuvenating my wise old woman sub personality.'

'Fantastic.'

I gave her arm an extra squeeze. How can you knock someone who works so hard at being who she is?

'Bullshit, Jutta,' said Tammi, from behind me, 'why can't you drop all that jargon and just be straight for once?'

Ah. Like that, apparently.

Unnecessarily harsh, I felt. Luckily, Henry was there to save the day.

'That's rich, coming from you,' he joked. 'Why can't *you* be straight?'

Aha. I might be on the right track with Henry, then.

'I hear the pool men are coming up for lunch,' I stated casually.

Jutta positively glowed. I must be right about Vlad. Must remember to get Jutta on her own to check out all possibilities.

'Oh God, not more dancing,' Tammi grinned, 'got a decent pair of knickers on, Jutta?'

We all laughed, sat down and began to nibble the olives that Henry had thoughtfully placed on the table. Then, bless his cottons, he brought out a chilled jug of Pimms, and four glasses chinking with ice, so that by the time Joe and Vlad arrived, we were all very relaxed and engrossed in conversation.

'No, I think that New Labour were far more reactionary than the eighties Tories ever were, and that's been the problem,' Jutta was claiming, in a rather loud but charming way, and then looked embarrassed as the lads walked through the door onto the patio.

'Good day, ladies,' said Joe with a cheeky grin, while Vlad bowed deeply and simply said, '*Senhoras.*' Then they both went up to Henry and shook hands very warmly, before coming boldly round to kiss all of us women on the cheek, twice of course. Vlad led the way by kissing Jutta first, and holding on to both of her hands.

112

'Well, and how it is today, your lovely leg?' he said, concern clear in his voice. 'So unfortunate, the dancing to Tina Turner like that – the bar really should have rail across those evil steps.'

Jutta replied in coquettish terms, and then Vlad came around the rest of us with his warm brown eyes and genuine smile.

Rapidly followed by Joe, who went first to Tammi and then to Jutta, and last to me. I could barely look at him. Fortunately, Henry was in the kitchen calling to Vlad who had gone in to get a beer, so he didn't see that when Joe bent over to kiss me, his elbow just very faintly caught the outer limits of my left breast. It was one of those events that could have been either truly accidental, or else very well thought out and executed – very well thought out indeed. Anyway, whatever its intention, the effect was sheer electricity and once again I felt that I might betray myself by coming on the spot, but I managed a clear 'hello, Joe,' which I think sounded okay, although Tammi did look at me with an eyebrow raised. Although Jutta is by trade the expert on human nature and body language, I am far more wary of Tammi's astuteness, and I just looked back at her and then moved my gaze away.

'Sit down, Joe,' I said. 'Please, help yourself.'

'Pool first, then we can chill out while the chlorine works,' he replied assertively, and with that he went to get the vacuum and brushes out of the truck and began to work.

Vlad and Henry came out with the beers, and in fact Henry went down and helped out with the whole pool business, laughing and joking with a beer in his hand, while we went back to our conversation, although I'd have to say that it lacked a certain conviction now that at least two of us had been distracted by the presence of hunky young men.

'Shame there's no women working on the team,' I suggested to Tammi as I replenished our glasses. She gave me a sharp grin.

'Ah well, we're not all so needy that we're desperate for whatever we can get,' she said.

Before I could be indignant on Jutta's behalf, Tammi moved on. 'And anyway, I've signed up for a walk tomorrow, three hours on the west coast with a guide. She seemed very nice on the phone. Said there were quite a few women going.' She turned the lightest shade of pink. 'So I'll give that a go, and get out of your hair while you catch up with Rosie.'

By the time the lads joined us, we were glowing with the heat and the Pimms, and just relaxed enough to no longer feel embarrassed or awkward. Henry went into the kitchen and emerged with a large tray full of salad and some stuffed eggs, as well as some very large spicy sausages which he had cooked and kept hot in the oven. I couldn't resist taking one of those, and looked Joe straight in the eye while I ate it.

I feel a bit daft now confessing such ridiculous behaviour, but there you go.

We had a thorough debrief of the debauchery of two nights ago, and all agreed that it had been great fun and we must do it again sometime. Joe said it had been a while since he had been in such charming company, and he was careful to include Tammi as he swept his gaze around. She was darting looks at me left right and centre, and when we divided inevitably into smaller group conversations, she, Joe and I ended up talking about concepts of freedom and equality, and Joe stated again what a pleasure it was to be with women who were both attractive and intelligent, so unlike the types you sometimes find out here on holiday, or even the expats. Tammi was becoming bold by now and winked at me more than once. Henry, Jutta and Vlad were entrenched in a conversation about the comparison between the brain of a fish and the brain of a mammal, and how it was that dolphins were so amazingly a blend of the two. Jutta was discussing the possibility of dolphin therapy and what that might entail.

By the time we had eaten, it was arranged that Henry will go fishing next Friday with Vlad. That still leaves him time to catch up with various members of my due family, and he will deserve a little respite by then. He and Vlad will be out all afternoon, and I arranged publicly with the girls that I will book a table at the Beach Bar for anyone who wants to come to late lunch on that day, and I know that Joe noticed.

I know because when I went into the kitchen to deposit a tray full of crocks and to fetch some much needed iced water, Joe came in behind me and just rested very lightly against my back and put his lips to my neck. I could feel his erection and for a split second I just wanted to lean back onto him. But I was together enough to remember where we were, and so just turned around to

114

face him and gave him a look. A look that should have said a firm no, but said instead 'not now, not here'.

'Sorry,' he whispered, 'I just couldn't help it.'

'Oh wow.'

Bang went my maturity and impending wisdom. I knew that he must have been able to see the lust in my eyes and feel it from the heat of my body. I followed my 'wow' with 'iced water,' and went quickly to the fridge. I had to get out as soon as possible or else I would have straddled him there and then.

He came out a few minutes later, looking composed. We all had water, and then Vlad and Joe went on their way and we said 'see you on Saturday if not before', and I spent the rest of the afternoon between the sunlounger and the pool, my thoughts on the lounger adding degrees to the naturally warm temperatures, and the water repeatedly cooling me down. Perhaps I should speak to someone about this, probably Tammi. Or I suppose I could contact Fenella and give her a bit of a preview of the personal coaching log that could be landing in her inbox soon.

Although this blogging lark is pretty therapeutic by itself, so we'll see.

So now we are about to have a quiet supper in. I'm fetching Rosie tomorrow and Jutta will probably want to come with me, partly because she is Rosie's godmother, and partly because she hasn't got the sensitivity not to.

I'll deal with that one in the morning.

rambling Rosie

april 17th 2010

I needn't have worried about anything, as it happened. The next morning saw Henry going out for a run, shorts, sweatband and all, very excited with himself. Both Jutta and Tammi were up at reasonable hours, Tammi had her walking plans, and Jutta also revealed that she had plans for the day, and would I mind if she didn't come to the airport. We then had a three witches breakfast out on the patio, as Henry had assured us he would be at least an hour.

'So,' said Jutta, tucking into a fresh mango, 'd'you think he's really interested?'

I was so shocked by the abruptness and frankness of this enquiry that I answered without hesitation.

'Well if his behaviour in the kitchen was anything to go by, then there really just isn't any doubt. Although I don't know what will happen when the girls come. I mean there's nothing like the younger version of the same bloodline to make a woman look old.'

Tammi tried to stop me halfway through this admission, but to no avail. I was off.

'Why would Vlad take any notice of your offspring, Izzie?' Jutta looked perplexed. 'And what do you mean, his behaviour in the kitchen?'

Too late, I realized my mistake. There was I being ever so selfish, and there was poor Jutta trying so hard to catch a man and I was supposed to be encouraging her and rooting for her, and instead I was just being as horny as hell over a lad half my age.

'Sorry, Jutta, I got confused.' She took another bite of mango, her eyes belying a level of thoughtfulness. 'Yes, I do think Vlad's interested. I mean he's very caring about your ankle, and you seem to get on so well in discussion. And he's very attentive to you.'

She wasn't to be fobbed off. And neither was Tammi. Who interjected.

'Come on then, Izzie, what happened in the kitchen? I know Joe went in after you. I noticed. Come on, spill the beans.'

116

And I did. In the sketchiest outline possible. In terms of what he did and said. Jutta's eyes widened and then she clasped her hand over her mouth.

'Oh shit, Izzie, do you want me to give you some assertiveness training to help you sort him out?'

Tammi gave an irritated sigh.

'For a psychologist, Jutta, you do get it so wrong,' she gloated. 'Izzie loved it – can't you tell? And now she's wondering whether to go the whole hog or not. Right, Izzie?' And then she did that thing with a fig that she'd done in the restaurant the other night.

At which point I came clean and revealed the shocking depth of my lust, my turmoil at the conflict between wishes and commitments. And my fears about Henry's insecurities, and how I couldn't possibly hurt him and yet how I am so in touch with only living once and therefore really being hedonistic and taking the bull by the horns in this life.

So to speak.

Naturally, both friends had a lot to say on the subject. Tammi was the one who was most on for me going for it, even though she and Henry are so close. She concluded,

'So how often is this going to happen to you from now on, Izzie? I mean, I'm not being funny, but you won't be pulling twenty-odd-year-olds forever. You're in transition, aren't you, a sabbatical so that you can research or write or chill, it's your fiftieth birthday. I mean, you're ripe for a change. And you do only live once. I don't think Henry will be hurt because he won't know anything about it. And anyway, you never know what he might get up to at some point.'

Jutta leapt in to reassure me.

'Don't be ridiculous. Henry would never be unfaithful to Izzie. For goodness sake, he never looks at another woman, not with any serious intent at least. And I think you should consider all factors very carefully, Izzie. You've been around the block a bit, and Henry's been really good to you. And the children.' She looked pointedly, daggers even. 'And yes, Rosie is coming today and then you'll see what's really important to you.'

'Goodness,' said Tammi, sweetly, 'that's fairly critical and prescriptive for someone so adept at being non-judgmental.'

'Oh fuck off, you can be so pious, Tammi. Believe me, I've got Izzie's interests at heart a lot more than you have. I mean, I am Rosie's godmother.'

Jutta smirked, but then flushed, conscious perhaps that she was on the edge of a catfight – not pretty.

And it was pissing me off.

'Okay, if it's going to cause these kind of problems, then my mind is made up. No more flirting.' I paused. 'Well, a little flirting, but that's as far as it goes. I am *not* going to be one of these women with a mid-life crisis.'

Even as I write that statement, I'm aware that this is about the third time I've protested on this subject this month, which is not good. 'And you're right, Jutta, we should be talking about you and Vlad.'

'I'll talk to you in the car,' said Jutta, face flaming, and not from the heat of the sun. 'On the way to the airport. I think I'd like to come after all.'

By now I was needing company like I needed a hole in the head.

'Actually, Jutta, will you mind if I go on my own to fetch Rosie – only I haven't seen her for so long and it would be nice to have a bit of private time just to catch up.'

Jutta was caught now between her own selfish needs, and the fact that, having publicly failed to be non-judgmental once this morning, she couldn't be seen to fail again; and she would need to be empathic for good measure.

'Of course. Insensitive of me.'

'But we'll catch up again later, hey? I'd really like that.' I gave Jutta a hug and told her that I loved her. And by the time I was ready to go out, relieved to be alone at last, Henry had come back, showered and was playing the guitar on the terrace, with Jutta draped on a sunlounger and gamely joining in with 'Streets of London'.

Deep joy.

I got into the car and accelerated away. As I sped up the motorway in the clear light of day, radio on, I had the deepest sense of being entirely alone. Whatever happens, I am responsible only to myself and only for myself. I have paid my dues. I am just a tiny dot, an earthling in the mega realm of space.

Then I ruminated on how I rush in headfirst with men, and thought about Rosie and her dad, Ken. Who I met at a self-development residential course, of all things. I was tired, I'd got Connie and I'd got Jon, and was working. I needed replenishment. Kids and a career, the feminist curse.

So, I booked myself in for the course in York, Sunday evening to Friday lunchtime. I had a great weekend with the kids first, so then I could go and personally develop without any guilt to get in the way.

Hoorah.

From the moment I arrived at the old stone built college, I felt at peace. The gardens were fab, flush with the red gold hues of an English autumn a la Keats, 'season of mist and mellow fruitfulness'.

Only no mist, just mellow fruitfulness, which suited me just fine.

I toured the gardens before braving the check in. I was nervous, so a stroll and a good breathing session was in order. I was literally stopping to smell the roses, enjoying the solitude as I bent over the bushes, when a voice boomed rich and deep in my ear.

'Beautiful.'

I nearly jumped out of my skin, and when I turned around, there was this gorgeous green-eyed man standing right behind me. As I was not at that point very self-developed, it being the beginning and not the end of the week, I instantly felt embarrassed and guilty as if I'd been doing something wrong. I muttered in agreement with him, then scuttled away to my room to have a quick un-personally developed cigarette.

I cleaned my teeth and chewed an extra strong mint, then made my way to Great Hall, for registration.

I'd been on a few teachers' conferences before, but this was different. We were given name badges. I hate name badges. If you pin them on your chest, that's where everyone looks, so they kind of say, 'Hello Izzie' to my left bosom, and then I always want to say, 'What do you think I should call the other one?'

I registered, donned the name badge, collected a folder full of information, and grabbed a coffee. I leafed through the timetable and course brochure from the folder. I mulled over the prospect of 'Total rebirthing: discover the baby within', and, 'To be the self that one truly is: the T group experience'. This made me think of T bone, as in a large steak, and then I felt embarrassed as I was just sure that Great Hall was full of vegetarians who could

119

read my thoughts. 'Left hand art workshop' appealed quite a lot, as did 'Bioenergetics; unlocking body armour'.

Lots of people seemed to know each other. Many wore brightly coloured outfits and some looked like they'd never left the late sixties, in flowing gowns and shapeless trousers, drinking herbal teas and spring water. As I scanned the room, I realised I was searching out the other wallflowers.

I managed not to mingle with a single soul before the introductory plenary session. Someone welcomed us to the conference and went through the domestics, the purpose and various other details, and I began to wonder what I was doing there: everyone seemed so earnest. Our first task was to find a 'Home Group', a group to attach to for the week. Home Groups met twice daily, morning and evening, so that you could 'process' what was going on for you. It was going to be safe, secure, and the very seat of the 'real' learning. I felt like a fraud, as I just wanted to be outside with the flowers again. I realized that actually, I just needed a holiday, a break from what seemed like years of learning and working and feeling responsible and guilty, in equal shares, for the two unfortunate young beings who were my children.

I should just have gone to the seaside.

On instruction from the facilitator, everyone leaped to their feet and six clearly seasoned personal developers walked calmly to stand beside big sheets of paper dotted around the room, with 'Home Group' and the name of a flower written on. There was Rose, which I rejected because it was too thorny, and I wasn't going to admit to that side of my character at this short notice; Iris, beautiful yet droopy; Pansy, far too wilting; Daffodil, relentlessly bright and cheerful; Poppy, kind of tempting, but probably not for the right reasons; Tulip, instantly sending me into song. There was some determined mingling going on, while I loitered at the edge of the room.

I caught the eye of one other person, a tall willowy creature, eyes like rabbits in car headlights, and, given that I'm at my best when someone else seems in a worse state than me, I braved an introduction.

And that's how I found Jutta. I liked her straight away *because* she was as frightened as I was, and at that stage she was training to be a counsellor. We joked about setting up a rebel home group and calling ourselves the Wallflowers, setting the tone for much irreverence to come. Eventually we got taken under the wing of someone from Poppy who obviously thought we looked like more fun than her group. She was fat, fair and probably in the running for gallstones, and was very much into *Transactional Analysis* – TA. I now know this is a form of psychological analysis, but back then she seemed to talk in riddles.

'I know I'm a bit forward, but it's because I've got a Hurry Up Driver,' she confided, and Jutta and I nodded knowledgeably. 'I used to be Please Others, but I've done a lot of work on that.'

Clearly, she was quite mad, which was good enough for me.

The Home Group then spent the rest of the evening making its rules. We would meet twice a day, morning and evening, and we would take joint responsibility for facilitation. We agreed to commit to the group, and to take turns in speaking. We would not divulge confidences made in the group sessions, and we would not gossip about each other.

That agreed, Jutta and I went to the bar and began to discuss everybody. We giggled about the language being used and kept affirming each other's views with 'I hear what you're saying', or 'Wow, you seem to be in a difficult place right now', and then snuck out round the back to have a cigarette.

When we came back in, there was Ken, looking round the room. When he saw me, he came over and offered us both a drink.

'How's it going?' he purred, as he put a bottle of wine and three glasses on the table.

I was awed by him, those green eyes. I thought he was going to be very straight and woolly, but as the evening wore on I relaxed my view. He told some quite unsound jokes, yet wasn't he, as a trainer, supposed to be very right on? On the other hand, how nice that he wasn't precious and steeped in jargon. I went to bed feeling a bit better about the whole place, and although I didn't yet know it, I'd made a friend for life in Jutta.

Over the next couple of days I went to workshops and found some more interesting than others; I swam in the college pool, bliss; I wrote a journal, the only time I ever have before this one; but I never got on with the Home Groups, they left me feeling bruised and uncertain. Our group had two empty chairs in it, 'Happy Chair' and 'Sad Chair', and if you wanted to talk anything through in those moods, you were supposed to sit in those chairs. I just felt stupid. On the third evening, I talked a little about Constantine and Attila, and someone encouraged me to talk to a cushion as if it were my Mother. When I got angry with him for being a perv, he just said to me, 'You see, you *are* angry – you want to hit the cushion'. I just looked at him, and said very quietly but firmly, 'I am angry, but it's with you, and it's you I want to hit, right in the middle of your stupid face.' I left the room then, and it was at that point that I felt I really was already okay, just a bit mixed up in some ways.

And let's face it, at least I'd given them something to 'process'.

It was that evening that Ken found me outside, again, sitting on the grass by the flowers, having a quiet fag and thinking about what a mess I'd made of things, yet that it was also okay, I really was doing my best. I was just tired.

Ken went to the bar and returned with the inevitable bottle of red. I told him all about my past, my children, my love for them, my feelings of inadequacy, all of it. He listened calmly and seemed to understand. When he said to me that I was beautiful, I believed him, and it was only a few steps from there to bed.

I went to his room in my nightshirt and jacket. We hadn't even kissed, but I knew that sex with him would be fabulous. I felt fully alive for the first time in ages. I wasn't pretending to be anyone, not hiding in my own shadow, nothing to fear, nothing to fake. He had several candles burning in his room, and the delicious smell of verbena incense. I slipped into bed beside him and we made love, our hands, mouths and bodies merging into a sea of mutual pleasure. Afterwards, we drank champagne which he had ready in a cooler box, and then we made love again. And again. Then we slept the sleep of the well laid, and it wasn't till morning that the issue of birth control even crossed my mind.

This time when I found I was pregnant, I didn't panic. Keats' autumn gourd had swollen, ready to provide new life in the following summer. I felt that it was meant to be, that this babe was made in love. I let Ken know straight away, and made it clear that I had no expectations of him, but he wanted to be involved. We developed an easy blend of casual yet committed relationship; he listened to me when I talked, held me when I cried, and spoke to Rosie through my pregnant belly, which he loved and thought to be beautiful. He kept a detailed photographic log of the whole pregnancy. He would encourage me to express my feelings as I stood naked, my ripening body tall and proud, and he saw this as therapeutic. He catalogued the whole gestation. We made love often and for hours at a time, lazily, passionately. I knew my baby was Rosie from the minute I knew I was pregnant and when I bought her anything, I bought it in yellow.

I gave birth to the most beautiful little girl on earth. The midwife was quite happy to accommodate my crawling round on all fours while Ken read poetry to me and played pan pipe music to accompany Rosie's entrance into the world. I loved her, just as I had while she grew within me.

Jutta agreed to be Rosie's godmother. She wanted to be my birthing partner, but refused to be there with Ken. She thought his sleeping with me on the course was unethical. She distrusted how he had the candles burning ready, the champagne on ice.

She might have been right.

Jutta went on to train in all kinds of amazing therapies, including transpersonal psychology, an innovation, apparently, where if you want to you can analyse and learn from every second of your encounters. I find this logistically baffling, you'd have to spend your whole life in therapy, wouldn't you, to have enough time to rerun the previous hour or day. Then you'd have to do the same again with the therapy session, so that you'd always be reliving, like a kind of horrific Groundhog Day. But then, I'm not as qualified as Jutta, so what do I know? She's practised on me relentlessly, and I was a case study for two of her diplomas and one Master's course. I couldn't have hoped to have a better friend, and neither could I have hoped to have a better daughter than my lovely Rosie.

And actually, that's true of Connie, really, as well.

While I was in the relationship with Ken, I enjoyed having Connie back living with me. Ken believes in family values, though he didn't think it a good idea to move in with me – after all, as a therapist, he knew better than anyone how important it was to have our own space – but he spent loads of time with us at weekends and was extremely generous, in a material sense. Not only did he give me maintenance money, he actually made me a lump sum payment from a legacy that some appreciative client had apparently left him (rather unusual but all above board, he assured me). That's how I was able to buy my first house with only a fairly small mortgage, a three bed semi in the outskirts of Birmingham.

Ken and I lasted for three years before his personal development needs led him to travel around the world in search of inner enlightenment and an exploration of the Buddhist faith. He always wrote to us all from wherever he was. He finally returned and settled down in a communal set up near Totnes, Rosie spending all the holidays with him. She's turned out to be a well rounded young woman, pursuing a career as a teacher.

My memories filled the distance between the villa and the airport, and got me nicely into Rosie mode. I parked up ten minutes before the plane was even due, so I knew that it would be a good half an hour before she came through. I went inside and bought myself a magazine from the bookshop – 'She' – an extravagance at twice the UK price, and ordered a milky coffee from the coffee bar. The choice of magazine was intentional, as two front page headlines really intrigued me – 'Why Older Women Need Younger Men', and 'How to Make Your Skin look Ten Years Younger', as if the whole caboodle was designed especially for me.

By the time I went to look for Rosie, I knew, for the hundredth time, that I needed to drink lots of water, do a daily headstand, use some very expensive creams, detox four times a year, stop smoking, cut down wine, and stay out of the sun. I also knew that the ideal lover, physiologically speaking, can be twenty-five years younger than a woman. Henry is ten years younger than me, and I should really be settled with that. But it was also gratifying to read of women not much younger than me having satisfying relationships with men in their *twenties*, so I felt a little less guilty about fancying a man young enough to be my son. It's all about hormones – we women just mature well like the best wines, while men can either do well or can err to the wrong side of a ripe cheese.

I positioned myself so that I would get earliest view of my girl, and noticed again the differences between English and Portuguese women travelling. The English women split into their two camps, either very heavily made up, usually blond hair and dressed up to the nines in a kind of 'smart but casual' kind of way; or, as I know I have commented before, go for comfort with a giant C, whatever that takes. Whereas the Portuguese, particularly the more mature women, look well co-ordinated – often in black, cream and caramel shades, simple or extravagant high quality gold jewellery, firm hairdos tamed with spray, full make-up, scarves, gloves and matching shoes and handbags.

I wonder whether deep down I do in fact have some Portuguese blood in me, for although I wouldn't dress in quite such an old-fashioned way, I do fancy that my style resembles more the Portuguese than the English class. And Zé in the local *garafeira* – wine shop – did say that I have a very good accent considering I have only just arrived, so to speak, when I say my *faz favor, obrigada, bom dia, como estas?* and so on. I think I will maybe research my family tree when I get back.

I spotted Rosie straight away, tall like me but not so statuesque; more elm tree like, with a long slim body, strong yet with a touch of fragility that bends to the winds of change. Her hair looked positively golden, shiny and well cut, long yet shaped. She was wearing a pair of very low slung purple velvet flared trousers, a black ruched T-shirt and a divine short waisted plum velvet jacket. She had on a pair of wedges, and carried a deep purple suede shoulder bag. Even from where I was I knew that her fingers and toes would be wonderfully manicured and pedicured respectively. I heard my own intake of breath when I saw this stunning creature who was my daughter.

So many things went through my head. She's beautiful. She's me at her age. She looks so sexy. She looks so thin. She looks tired. Pride, love, fear. Questioning the fear: she's my flesh and blood, nothing to be worried about, she's a survivor. Yet at that sneaking hint of disquiet, just enough to make my heart skip a beat. And a tiny sense of guilt. Yet I had nothing to feel guilty about. So I left her a lot with her dad when she was growing up, so what? He's a very well worked out individual. I shook my unease away.

When she looked up and saw me, I smiled instantly, my forebodings swept away into an enthusiastic wave. Rosie's face lit up, eradicating the slightly dark shadows under her eyes that I had discerned. I shuffled further towards the front of the waiting group: I felt almost as if I lived here, my second time in one week at the airport, picking up guests. *Muito bem*, as the Portuguese would say, very good.

Rosie reached me in no time, gave a great grin and in seconds we were hugging, so closely, and it was like I'd only seen her yesterday, rather than the six months that it was in reality. Christmas had been spent with her father and New Year in Cyprus with some friends.

'Mum,' she said, 'you look great.'

'So do you, honey, so do you,' I said, and I meant it. She'd been travelling, so the dark circles were to be expected. 'How was your flight?' We exchanged catch-up trivia then, until we were safely in the car, Rosie's leather bags trimly placed in the boot.

'So how's it going, Mum, how's it really going?' Rosie had the earnest intensity of her father, but somehow more so. 'I mean, a month's a hell of a long time. And it was great of Henry, but, you know, it could all get very boring or something. So how is it really?'

She made me want to laugh, and she also made me want to tell her the truth. I settled for compromise.

'Well, so far it's been mostly really good,' I said, 'apart from one awful game of golf and the interference of Jonah Jim.' I caught her up on both of these blots, and she nodded sagely when she heard about James' memos.

'Daft old fart,' she said. 'Is he coming, by the way?'

'Not sure to be honest,' I replied. 'Happily for us, he's been delayed by the ash cloud, and I know he wants to do some golfing, so even if they get here they're going to stay at the Meridien at Penina. All very posh, and means we only get to see him for one day.'

'Great,' she smiled. 'So the rest has been okay?'

'Yes, fab. Tammi and Jutta are playing reasonably nice. We had such a laugh the other night, great night out, Jutta ended up making a spectacle of herself at the Praia bar, but she's made a good recovery.' I grinned at the memory. 'And we've met one or two nice local people.' I thought of Joe, and wanted to say 'and the pool man is just gorgeous, about your age, and has got the hots for me.'

But instead, as I formed the sentences in my brain, I realized again a most unwelcome stab of jealousy. *About your age.* What if I turned out to be right? Joe would of course fancy Rosie to bits. The best of my good looks with her father's lovely eyes, and a body to die for. And I would be revealed for the sad old woman that I am becoming. I shuddered and for one second closed my eyes, opening them just in time to pull away from a Portuguese car that seemed to want to embed itself in our boot.

'What's up, Mum?' Rosie looked concerned. 'You look like you've seen a ghost.'

'I'm fine, Rosie, I'm fine,' I smiled determinedly and turned the subject to her.

'But tell me about you. How is Steiner? I'd imagine it suits you down to the ground. I'd love to have taught at one of their schools. How's it going?'

For the rest of the journey I let Rosie prattle on and focused on her, determined not to be so damned twisted all because of a young upstart of a pool man who, let's face it, probably tries it on with all his clients and is having a laugh at my expense or something.

Or a bet. How cruel would that be.

So by the time I got back to the villa, I felt tense beneath the pleasure of seeing Rosie. I settled her into the villa two doors up with we'd taken for all the progenies. She changed and went off to the bathroom for what seemed like hours, typical gorgeous young woman spending so much time on how she looks. She said how lovely it was to see me and there were a few things she thought she might talk to me about if she gets the chance. I think I was just a little bit lukewarm in my response, because then she quickly said that it was nothing important. And now I feel as if something is not quite right, but I can't for the life of me think what might be wrong or why I feel that it is.

No doubt we'll have plenty of time to catch up. Connie and John are here on Thursday, they will taxi from the airport, and Stef and maybe Chris are due any day, so we have a couple of days to ourselves before they come.

Great.

purging

18th April 2010

Just as everything was going so well life has come and slapped me round the back of the head. I need to collect my thoughts. Here goes.

I started the day with a walk to the village; it's quite hot now in the daytime so mornings are great. I love the smell of mimosa and jasmine just as I get into the lived-in bit. I saw the goatherd as well, he nodded at me and I waved. And I bought fresh rolls, as usual, little plump white pillows full of flavour. I walked around on the beach, trying to get back to that tiny dot feeling, to remember that the ocean has been there for squillions of years, and will be there way after the drama of my life has played out, and I breathed in its ions as deeply as I could before making my way back 'home'. I've seen Tammi, she's up and about and off for a run, Jutta is still in bed, or at least in her room, and Henry won't surface for a while. So it's a good little space to collect those old thoughts.

As I said, yesterday I thought Rosie looked thin but well, hazel eyes just slightly duller than they should be, but hey. I understood that she'd been staying over with Ken, who has always adored her, and imagined that this would have been pleasant for her. Yet I knew that something jangled, and I wasn't sure what.

When we got back here from the airport, once settled, Rosie had emerged from her bathroom stint wearing bikini and a sarong which framed the top of her willowy long legs, gently casing her perfectly shaped bottom and, between her hips, a table top flat stomach, pierced, of course, and spray tanned in a booth. She looked great, and after I'd had my blogging session and gone out to the patio, I'd said so.

'Rosie, you look great – stomach to die for.' She looked at me, straight on, and said the strangest thing.

'Why do women say that, Mum?'

'What do you mean?' Off she was again, intense. There was me just using an expression, and Rosie had taken me so literally.

'This "to die for" business. It's so annoying. You're supposed to be a feminist, and here you are talking about dying just to have a flat stomach. Do you realise just how much pressure that all puts on women these days? Have you looked around and seen all these thin sticks on the telly and in the mags, this bloody obsession with weight?'

Well, that shut me up a bit. I put my arm out to touch her, to let her know I was only being light-hearted, but she flinched, pulled back from my touch.

We passed through the moment, came back to the villa, and joined Jutta and Henry for food and drink, which was lovely. They caught up and Rosie told us all about her new job at Steiner, and I watched to check that she ate well, which she did. And she's passionate about those children, believes in getting to them when they're forming, the crucial time. Her aim is to develop all her children in a most creative way.

Rosie has a week's carefully negotiated leave, difficult in term time (though for Rudolf's disciples flexibility is the order of the day). She spent the weekend before the leave, on an educational/self-development weekend with a painting group. Ken had paid, apparently, *dear old Daddy*, she said, only with a certain amount of venom in her voice. I noticed she hardly drank any wine, whereas I found myself having quite a lot, to try and relax. She gave me a present from Ken.

'He said it's just a token, Mum, so I thought I'd give it to you now.'

She handed me an exquisitely wrapped parcel, maybe four by six, sage paper and silver ribbon, with a little card attached with S.W.A.L.K written on in very neat handwriting – *sealed with a loving kiss*. Something we used to do with each other. I felt uneasy. I looked at Henry and raised an eyebrow. He looked quite content, the inevitable red wine in hand, and he was muttering to Tammi, something about waxing, and what did she think to fashions in that department, so he didn't really seem very interested in my gift.

Anyway, I opened it, and it was a divine bracelet, orange and crimson crystals, plain in design and stunning in execution, reflecting light left right and centre and generally being a dazzling piece.

'It's gorgeous, how lovely.' I put it on, smiled at Rosie, who smiled back. A little tightly.

'Yes, well, he always did adore you. He's always telling me about how I was conceived, you know, your time at York and Ripon St John, the college and that workshop. I think he might have stayed with you forever if you'd let him.'

I don't know if it was just me, or what – everything seemed to have taken on this edgy meaning, I was uncomfortable, so I resolved to have a proper chat.

At that point, Tammi had arrived back by taxi from her expedition with the walking group. She was high as a kite, clearly invigorated. She went and showered and joined us for sunbathing and nibbles. Apparently the walk had been spectacular, from slightly inland, a place called Barão São Miguel, not far from here, down to the coast line and the cliff tops. She described eucalyptus woods, magnificent views, sparkly seas, but was also full of excitement about the variety of people she'd met. She looked me in the eye.

'And you'll never guess – I met someone who knows you.'

'Who?' I didn't know who she was on about.

'A woman called Jean. She was in the pub apparently the other night and you and Henry were there, must have been before we came, she said you introduced yourself.'

To my shame, especially now, my internal response had been trite, just stopping myself saying out loud the words Salad Dodger, or Thorntons Tart. How could this woman disturb me so much? And now she went walking, damn her. What a great life she must have.

Here I went again, intelligent, fortunate woman, harbouring a well of envy, resentment, meanness.

Inadequate. Fattist. Trivial.

I shook myself, found myself dismissive.

'Oh right. Yes, I don't really know her, we were on the same plane. What does she do then?'

'Apparently she works part-time as a Pilates teacher. She helps out in some charity venture as well, walks a lot. She was really nice.'

I was just about to go bitchily down that road of wondering how someone so chubby could teach Pilates, when I remembered what Rosie had said to me. And had been right. Everything was churning in me now, self-doubt, concern about Rosie, too many voices in my head. So I shut up, listened to Tammi and bade my time, waiting to speak to Rosie. I resolved to go round to the progeny house later on, once the social business of the day was over

Which is how it was that I happened upon Rosie later with two fingers down her throat and head over the toilet bowl. I'd walked round, after dusk, called her name, and when she didn't answer I let myself in through the open patio windows. I heard a noise which I thought was her in distress, headed towards the bathroom, and there she was. Making herself sick.

'Rosie.' I thought I'd whispered, but she turned her head around very quickly, for a second, between hurls, and I saw that her eyes were teary and red, and she let go one more horrible expunging vomit. I knelt at her side, holding her hair back out of her face, my other arm around her back, saying, 'there, Rosie, there, it's okay,' or something like that, and then she was in my arms, sour breath wafting in my nostrils, wet face against my shoulder, and we both cried and hugged, and I just said her name over and over.

It was one of the most intimate moments we've had since she was a small girl.

Afterwards, we were both slightly awkward. We got up from our now unseemly position on the bathroom floor, she rinsed her mouth, we passed round a flannel for her and for my shoulder, all the usual female cleaning up after ourselves type stuff.

We talked, then, quietly into the night. She told me all sorts of things which leave me reeling a little. I thought I was done with feeling guilty when it came to my children, but when she revealed to me how much she missed me over the years, I ached. If only I'd known.

Rosie told me stories, lots of cameos of things that had happened between Ken and her. They seemed to revolve around her father's obsession with freedom of the body, self-development and photography. It turned out that not only was the gestation of Rosie documented on film, but almost her whole life.

Much of it, naked.

Did I know that Ken was quite comfortable walking around in the house naked? Well, yes, but I didn't know that he continued to do this as Rosie blossomed into adulthood. Did I know that he had photographed her naked, right up until the age of fourteen, and that even then she had to really insist that he didn't, and by then he had already taken photos where she had felt embarrassed and humiliated? No, I bloody well didn't. Did I know that he had had her model naked for an art class, only a year ago, against her better judgment and under considerable pressure, without telling her that he would be a member of that art class? Did I know that he emphasised continually the importance of the form of the female body, showed her nude pictures he'd taken of other women, all of them reed slim? No, I didn't. Did I know he'd asked her not to tell me, better not, in case I didn't understand?

I felt furious, scared, confused, tried to create a picture of what was unfolding, the blur between Ken's libertarianism and his overstepping of personal boundaries.

'Did he ever touch you?'

I had to know.

Rosie shook her head.

'Not really, mum, only affectionate pats on my knee in the car, a pat on the bum too many, an arm around me – and he is my dad. So no, he didn't physically abuse me, if that's what you mean. Really, he just loves me, but now, with help, I realise he's not appropriate. When I was younger, he made me feel self-conscious all of the time and that I must be slim and model like, and I just wanted him to stop talking about sex all the time and telling me how beautiful I am.'

Suddenly the memories of Ken the tutor sleeping with his student, inheriting money from a client, reconfigured into a more sinister shape. Ken *was* inappropriate; Ken *is* inappropriate. And his stupid, liberal, arty-farty 'authentic' living had pressured our girl into a painful and destructive self-consciousness.

She asked me never to speak of this again, which I foolishly promised her, because after all, I just might need to talk to someone: then again, I just might need to go and cleave Ken's head open with an axe, the miserable, selfish, bastard.

But for now, I feel that I've purged myself a little just through writing it down. We ended our evening fairly rationally. And collecting thoughts here has given me perspective. Ken has taken at least a little emotional advantage of Rosie in the past, but it's over now; she is having some counselling help, so feels that she is getting her bulimia under control; me finding out, apparently, is a good thing, as I was the last person to know who really needed to know. Her trip to Totnes, en route to Portugal, she tells me, was a confrontative event, not an Art Class at all, and she will not be seeing Ken again for the foreseeable future. She feels that overall, her experiences have made her into a deeper person who will be a better teacher, and actually is just glad it wasn't any worse. So from Rosie's point of view, things are on the up.

Things are on the up.

I can't address anything more just now. Rosie has asked me to trust her to sort herself out, and trust her I will. I will shelve my feelings, because to be honest I can't even verbalise them fully yet, and will leave Rosie with some control over what happens next.

I had two large *macieras* before lights out, which rendered me unconscious, though I don't think I slept.

Fifty years of life loom nearer. I've had my share of ups and downs. You know what they say – what doesn't kill you makes you stronger. They also say in Buddhism, so I understand, that life only throws at you what it knows you can take. I've probably distorted the message, so that the downside of that seems to be the stronger you are, the more shit gets thrown your way. Maybe I should have been less strong, more vulnerable, not chosen to deal with stuff. On the other hand, maybe what happens to one's children is going to happen anyway, so that somewhere in the universal order their soul chose you as their mum, because they knew that when push came to shove, there you'd be, strong.

I just don't know. But for now, life seems to be only about the important things, and everything about this month before today seems trivial and banal.

bewitched, bothered and bewildered

april 19th 2010

I'm flummoxed, well and truly. I spent most of yesterday feeling dazed, hazy, and lazy. Rosie acted as if nothing had happened, and there was I committed to never speaking of her revelation again. I went through it in my head, tried to normalise things. Nothing too physically intrusive, yet psychologically weird, and more than inappropriate. Selfish. Destructive. Harmful.

Ken being bloody well in the moment, I suppose. And could Rosie be remembering things wrong, that strange false memory syndrome?

No. Of course she couldn't.

I spent the day swimming, sitting around, walked to the village with everyone, spoke to Stefan on the phone. He apologized for his tardiness and failure to get in touch, which meant I didn't have to confess to having totally forgotten that he too was supposed to be arriving late on Tuesday night. I mean, it's all very well those tales of mothers of infants leaving the baby on the bus, but you're supposed to grow out of it aren't you, and shouldn't really leave the adolescent son forgotten at the airport.

Anyway, I was off the hook there, if a little disturbed at my errant memory.

So he's coming tomorrow now, though hasn't yet got a flight.

Not with Jon, who got really stuck in Lahore. Only two planes out over the last month, apparently, and both involved in volcanic ash disruptions. Now he is travelling overland somehow, and, long story short, no one really knows where he is.

But Connie arrived, and Henry kindly fetched her from the airport, and then I got two big surprises.

One, Connie herself, who seems to have metamorphosed from dormouse to diva, all on the journey today apparently. Vibrant plum hair instead of brown – she wonders what her husband will say, he doesn't know yet – and revealing to her sister (poor timing actually, in a way, but never mind) a drawer full of exotic new La Perla underwear, and two very sassy dresses.

134

'You know, Mum, if you're going to be fifty, then I'm well into my thirties (thirty-two, actually, they just don't appreciate how young that is) and I need to spruce up a bit.' I kissed her impulsively on the cheek. Yes, honey, I thought, you go for it. You've done too much, much too young – married with the kids when you should be having fun.

Good old Madness.

And her biggest surprise for me, and this was a smackerooney, was bringing Mother with her. Attila. My mum. Helena Vivienne Malleen.

I had been, as I said, out of touch, so when I saw her come out of the taxi, my mouth must have gaped all over. She looks mellower to me, though I wonder if there is a thin veil over my eyes, that seems to be turning everything softer. At any rate, I was so pleased to see her that I nearly cried. And she too with smartly cropped hair, a tiny tinge of purple on the iridescent silver. She tells me she has enrolled in the Open University, women's studies.

What is going on? All these women, flesh and blood, all going through something, and bringing it here.

I'm probably not making much sense. I'm tired, to be honest, and so much has happened yet there seems little more to put down in writing. Henry has saved the day food wise again, going off early to the supermarket and to the fish market in Lagos, serving us all garlic prawns and huge salad. He has also, bless him, reserved our table at the Beach Bar for tomorrow, adding on and taking off as people fall in or out.

I've just had a fag, bliss. I can hear my name being called, thank heavens there are enough people to dilute everything so that I can just cruise along. Tomorrow I will focus, my last day of being forty-nine. Tammi always says don't sweat what you can't control: Jutta constantly tells me to look after the small things, there are no big things. With these thoughts, I'll go and join in the evening and try and make sense from my confusion.

conga moments

april 20th 2010

Bells again, this time attached to pigs, by the sound of them. A stream of sunlight sneaking through half closed shutters. For a moment I just lay there in the balmy tranquillity of my waking, enjoying the hinterland between sleep and wakefulness, light as a feather. A really deep pig grunt assailed me through the tinkling, jolting me one step closer to consciousness.

And the certainty that pigs don't usually tinkle.

I opened my eyes, saw Henry next to me, mouth wide open, snoring. Heard the goats outside.

Remembered where I was and what was going on.

I am here in the Algarve, on the last day of my first half century of life. It seems unbelievable that I could have lived this long, be this age, not in the wrinkle ageing sense, but just in the reality factor that I have lived for nearly a whole fifty years, interacting and reproducing, just being alive.

I leaped out of bed and decided that come what may today, this was cause for celebration. I padded downstairs and went out onto the patio. I could hear those surefooted goats coming down the hillside, the noise of an occasional car passing. I made my salute to the sun, three times, stretched and appreciated life. Then I made a herbal tea and just sat and drank it, enjoyed the air. I am really quite excited about what might happen next, and the melting pot of my family and friends can only bring me joy, can't it, because however dysfunctional we are, we're all we've got, and the past is the past.

Mother's arrival really has pleased me. For all these years, although I have technically loved her, I haven't always felt close to her. We've both been so busy *doing*, that we've rarely just spent time together, *being*. I think I have been trying to be other, that despite all my responsibilities and achievements, I have seen me as youthful and young, and her as old, as if across some kind of divide. Yesterday, when she arrived, I knew deep in my soul that it was she who would understand my maternal angst and trials, and that it was she who had always looked out for me in the best way she knew how. And in her purple hint of a tint, I saw her

136

youthfulness, and in her newly formalized learning, her brightness, her enthusiasm.

I leaped onto the bicycle that resides here in the car port and cycled down to the crossroads, waved at the men in hats in the bus stop, and went and mooched at the fruit van. It was replete with masses of juicy ripe oranges, so I bought three kilos, which filled my bicycle basket, turned around and pedalled back to the villa. I took them inside and squeezed them, every one, the juice of the tender flesh pouring prolifically and freely into the jug below.

Jutta was up next, and within ten minutes, the whole family arrived, so we took out the orange juice onto the patio and Henry made toast, Tammi brewed coffee, and we brought out the condiments, all sitting around.

'You look fab, Mother.' I smiled at Atilla.

'Thank you, Izzie.' She nodded at me, smiled back. 'You know, I wonder if you'd mind calling me Mum, or even Helena? 'Mother' always sounds so formal, and I don't really like it much.' She reached for the marmalade, took a great glob, and dropped it onto her toast. 'Connie always calls me Lena, you might even want to use that.' She squashed the marmalade down with a thick bladed knife, and spread it all over the toast.

I resolved that I would. I could understand that one, and if that's what she wants, then that's what I'll do.

'Okay, Mother, I'll do my best.'

'Thank you. Just as you must be thinking that you can't believe you're nearly fifty' – the old witch, she always could read my mind – 'I can't believe that I've been a mum for nearly fifty years. It doesn't leave me much time, so I'm really pleased to be getting on with my own things, at last.'

Awesome. Of course: she'd looked after me, then Connie, and I knew she'd been helping Connie with her two. I wanted to know more about her OU, about what she was up to. I smiled at her, noticed how hazel her eyes were.

'What a splendid day f-for f-f-fishing!'

Henry arrived with more toast. I'd quite forgotten about his outing, and it reminded me that today we were going to the Beach Bar for lunch. There's a zing in the air. And the caterers have rung to confirm tomorrow, we're not quite sure on numbers yet, still waiting on my boys.

Rosie is looking rosy, and ate a good slice or two of toast. I hope that now she's purged her mind, her body might be able to keep the toast down.

But I'm not going there.

We spent the morning sunbathing and swimming, again, and before we knew it, it was midday, time to shower and spruce, ready for our lunch date. Connie had disappeared somewhere earlier, something about exploring, and we said we'd meet her down there.

So off we trogged, Henry in his matelôt outfit, boarding pants and blue polo shirt, looking really excited, walking arm in arm with Tammi; Rosie and Jutta paired up, nattering and fondling the odd plant on the roadside; so I got to walk with Mother-Mum-Lena.

We linked arms.

'It's lovely to see you, you know.'

She smiled at me, looking fab in a long cool looking kaftan shirt and cream baggy trousers. She was carrying a fan – how clever – and wore a large floppy hat.

'Very stylish, Mo… Mum.'

'Well, as I said, I'm well into my last few years of life now, so I'm going to make them all for me. I've told Connie she's got to sort herself out now, I've got other fish to fry.'

Feisty Mum, always had an energetic soul.

'Oh?' I was curious now. 'What, the OU? How's it going?'

She smiled, a really soft aura smile. As it happened, we were just passing an old Portuguese man on a moped coming up the road, and she waved at him, and he waved back. Like she had some magic dust around her.

'Well yes, I love it. We've been looking at the Second World War, and how women got pushed about into the workplace and then back into the home, to suit the needs of the men at any given time. And housework expanding, being developed as an all consuming occupation, gadgets invented not to save us time, but to make us do more of it. More and more must have products to keep us busy. I love reading Betty Friedan, all that stuff.'

Fab. I was just about to go into *The Feminine Mystique* with her, that whole feminist analysis, when she surprised me again.

'And you might as well know, I've met someone on the summer school at Stirling. They call it a summer school, but they start them in April. He's called Ted, works on the rigs, he's about to retire and wants me to go on a cruise. I've said yes.'

I was gobsmacked.

'You're probably gobsmacked.'

Witch again.

'If you don't like it, it's tough titties.' She quickened the pace. I pulled her arm.

'How could I not like it? I think it's brilliant.' I threw my arms around her, and we hugged. There was the toot of a horn, the little Portuguese man passing us again on his motorbike, smiling broadly at the English abroad. Like he'd turned round specially.

'So when did you decide all this then?'

Mum cleared her throat.

'Not sure really. I'd been getting bored for a while. Then one evening, there I was having done Connie's ironing, getting ready to babysit while she went out, sitting doing my crossword, realised that crosswords were not enough. There was one word I was trying to get, the clue was an anagram of "tear bile". I thought it must be liberate, but it wouldn't fit. And then Mike walked past, and said, "Oh Helena, you've written 22 Across as 'carpe deum' – did you want to write that God is a fish, or should it be 'carpe diem'?"

'He was right, of course, so I changed it, and got my "liberate" in. Thought what a pompous ass Mike was, even if he was right. Decided that liberate would be a very good thing to do for myself, and show him that I have a brain too. As I say, I knew time was speeding up for me now, and Henry called to talk about this birthday idea and that kind of made it more official: you were going to be fifty. So I looked on the internet that night for courses, and there was an intake this January, so I applied.'

'Carpe diem.'

She laughed, and we chatted all the way to the Beach Bar. There was Vlad, stood outside, chatting to the others, and he greeted us in his lovely way, *pree-vee-et*, and making kisses all round, telling us that Joe was covering for him and might come down and have a coffee with us later. He and Henry said their goodbyes, Vlad telling me that they would 'have good time, don't worry, I know this place, I make sure that Enree gets off rocks alright', and off they went.

And then, there, at our table in the Beach Bar, was Connie – with Stefan! She had only nipped off to Lagos to meet him from the train and bring him back.

Deep bliss. Within minutes, we were all sat down, beers and rosé wine flowing, the waiters rubbing their hands with glee, I shouldn't wonder, at the inevitably lucrative few hours that lay ahead.

Stefan, in the event, had come on his own. Chris, whoever s/he had been, had obviously blotted their copy book in some way. It was just great to have him there. And Connie had gone to fetch him – wow.

The time flew. The Beach Bar location is, just as it suggests, right down on the beach, silver topped waves breaking gently over golden sands, cormorants diving for fish, lobster baked English bodies glowing on recliners here and there.

We ate, we drank, we made merry.

And then, over the main course, Stefan began the kind of conversation that only he can.

'This asparagus is fab, my absolute favourite. You know, they say that asparagus makes your piss smell, but that doesn't happen to me.'

Mother – Mum – wanted to know more.

'Who said that, and why?'

'Well, it's a common theory, apparently. But I've googled it, and there is now some agreement that it only affects a certain percentage of the population, and it doesn't happen to me.'

A young man at the next table turned around.

'Do you mind if I interject?'

'Not at all.' Stefan shared a huge smile with the unknown good looking interjector.

'Well, you're right, it seems to affect some people but not others, apparently. I can imagine that your piss would never smell.' His eyes twinkled. 'But have you ever tried beetroot – now *that* will make your piss turn pink.'

'Beetroot? Is that right?'

'Well, beetroot is known as a bit of a blood cleanser.' Jutta got her holistic penny worth in. The new young man nodded sagely.

'Yeah, try some beetroot. Take three or four beets and boil them, then you'll see.'

140

'Three or four? Not sure I can manage that.' Stefan laughed.

'Well you'll only have to try it once, I'm sure a man of your calibre will manage that.'

'So what other vegetables have these effects, then, I mean what is asparagus?'

The young man smiled.

'It's the same family as the sprout, you know, how sprouts grow on, like, a beanstalk.'

Stefan looked delighted. He then introduced the subject of the parsnip, and began a debate around it, and whether or not the roast parsnip has value in its own right, or whether it is doomed to be cast as a poor substitute for the roast potato, its softly cooked inner and scrunchy roast outer forever serving only to remind it's predatory human of what they could be having instead.

I lost the detail of this however as the young man's mum came back to the table while this unexpected conversation was occurring, because she was none other than Jean – the woman from the airport, the woman from the pub. Fatty. Salad Dodger. The Pilates teacher.

'Oh 'ello, alroight bab?' She waved cheerfully to me, her broad and shameless accent sounding really quite endearing now, and then Tammi turned round and was talking to her as well, and before we knew it we seemed to have merged our tables in a casual sort of way, and by the end of the whole afternoon, I had invited Jean, her friends and her son to my party.

I was three sheets to the wind by then, and didn't care. I thought that the magic of this place had cast a spell on us, because it was ages, years probably, since so many of my family had sat around like this, and I felt quite at liberty to make free with Henry's credit card and keep the rosé flowing. Connie had gone and metamorphosed into an elegant princess, her hair like a bejewelled silk around her face, which looked soft and gorgeous. She and I walked to the water's edge, hand in hand, talked about goodness knows what, agreed that it was great that she had come out on her own, tucked our skirts into our knickers and paddled.

Maybe we will talk again, sober, able to remember the details!

And then, at some point late on, Joe arrived. He was just there, drinking a large beer, looking fit and tanned as ever, and mixing in with everyone. He kissed me on both cheeks, and helped me keep some level of decorum at least by encouraging my creeping arms back to their sides as I went to fling them around his neck.

So there I was, with the most important people in my forty-nine years. One relationship specialist who couldn't keep a relationship to save her life; one seventy-two-year-old mother about to go on a cruise with an oil rig worker twelve years younger than her (I bow in her general direction), one daughter nearly fully purged of her self-depriving illness, one daughter going large in silky sexy underwear, shaking off her shackles, one son who could debate the power of the parsnip or the roots of Kleinian psychology, take your pick, and my smart gay Tammi who is just the most amazing woman in the world – nirvana. And to add the icing on the cake, new friends from unexpected sources, and my lovely young admirer.

I decided at some point to celebrate this wonder by leading a conga line up and down the beach, and had just done so with Joe right behind me, up very close indeed, the well-tipped bar staff turning up music for us and clapping along, when I saw Henry and Vlad coming into view and realized that six hours had passed at the Beach Bar.

And I hadn't thought about Henry at all.

He and Vlad both looked very suntanned, and content. They were carrying a bucket with some fish in, which Vlad was to take home, and told us about their afternoon on the rocks up the coast – the *rotzks*, as Vlad said – which apparently had been very calm.

We had coffee, and left the bar just before sundown. Henry reminded me that the caterers would want to be at the villa quite early, so it was probably a good thing not to have any more to drink. I said my goodbyes to Joe and the bar staff, who I also invited to the party, and Jean and her party all hugged and kissed us and promised to turn up tomorrow, so I hope they will.

And this is my last, calmer, time now, before that magic number comes and gets me.

Which I don't care about at all, now, strangely enough. It's just a number and anyway, you know what they say, you're only as old as the man you feel.

So will I be in my late thirties or early twenties this time tomorrow?

fifty

april 21ˢᵗ 2010

It's here. My 50ᵗʰ birthday. I awoke to bucks fizz and strawberries courtesy of Connie, who arrived at the bottom of my bed in a deep rose silk kimono.

'Happy Birthday, Mum,' she said, and kissed me. Then brought a tray from the ottoman on which she had rested it.

'Come on, sit with us,' I said and she did, swinging her legs up beside me on the king-size bed, and Henry went and fetched another glass, and they toasted me and we nibbled our strawberries and giggled, and then Connie got her beautifully wrapped gift for me from beside the bed, and presented it to me.

'Hope you like it,' she said, 'it's what you asked for.'

Since I couldn't remember what I'd asked for, it was a genuine surprise when I opened the beautiful paper to reveal a complete workout outfit, state of the art Nike in deepest purple, which will, I am sure, look very fetching on. There was also an exercise band, and then a little book – that poem, *When I am Old, I Shall Wear Purple*, which made me smile. Inscribed, 'My dear mum, unique, and fabulous. Enjoy.'

I felt a little lump in my throat, and looked at her, my firstborn, wondering what life would be like for her if she just cut loose.

Or for me.

Henry topped up our glasses, and soon Jutta and Tammi were in, with more champagne and sitting at the bottom of the bed, and lovely cards and pressies, one more workout suit, state of the art Nike (deep pink), a medicine ball and an exercise ball. A card, headlined 'This year, is also the 50ᵗʰ birthday of', and when I looked inside, it said 'the Pill!'

Clearly, I'd missed that one at the time☺.

Also, a beautiful photograph of the three of us that someone had taken only yesterday and managed to print out, and it was in a silver frame and they'd autographed it in the bottom right hand corner, my sisters under the skin, so that was fab.

Then Henry, slightly sheepishly, gave me his present. A Nike tracksuit. Pink and purple. And a pair of MBTs.

'You've given me so much, Henry, you've made this happen.' I kissed him.

And was remembering, now, how I'd asked everyone just to give me workout gear and such like.

In what seemed like a previous life.

Really, their presence, all these wonderful people, was my present, so all of these tangible gifts were extra. And they were fab – the poem, the photo, the holiday: I have a feeling I will remember this month in technicolor for the rest of my life.

We went downstairs and there was breakfast laid beautifully on the patio, my mother presiding over fresh croissants, figs, fruit juice, coffee, toast, eggs Benedict. Rosie and Stef were both there, and placing napkins and spoons in all the right places.

'Happy Birthday Mum!' Stefan gave me a bear hug of a greeting, squeezing me tight. He gave me a card, headline 'Congratulations, you can no longer die young', and a book, *Health and Fitness for the over Fifties*. Just as I was feeling slightly depressed by the well meaning tackiness that I think I had probably invited, he brought out an original edition signed vinyl copy of *Aladdin Sane*, one of my very favourite Bowie albums, to be treasured.

Mum was next with another book, *Fashion for the Over Fifties*, alongside a fab and beautiful Liberty silk scarf.

'You'll be wanting that, where you're going.'

I had no idea what she was on about – another surprise, or life in general? At any rate, it is a lovely scarf.

And then dear Rosie presented me with a beautiful handmade card, inlaid with pictures of us all, the children, me, Mum, the genetic grouping that is my family, and lovely silver writing on, a poem she'd written herself:

She's funny, she's feisty, she gave us her best,
And now that she's fifty it's time for a rest,
So let's raise a glass for our dear Isabelle,
A mother, a daughter, may your life proceed well.

The artistry made up for everything. And she gave me a pair of earrings, silver with mother-of-pearl inlay, quite delicate, very beautiful.

Henry brought me a little bundle of cards he'd brought with him. James and Mildred had sent me a cheque (typically

144

creative) for fifty pounds (typically imaginative, and seriously, typically mean.) A student had entrusted Henry with a pair of wrist weights, which he'd lugged all the way over here, a Nike workout outfit (purple, identical to the one upstairs) and a card signed by the whole group.

They say be careful what you ask for, you might just get it, and it seemed to me that my future was to be full of working out, but why? Seems wrong now. After breakfast, we went down to the café in town, as the caterers had arrived, early as planned, and we wanted to be out of their way for a while. Henry, bless, asked for the coffees in Portuguese – he has been studying my *Learn Portuguese in a Month* book.

'*Quatro sumos laranja, f-f-f-faz f-favor, e quatro galinhas fortes.*' He beamed at the woman behind the counter, and we clapped.

She guffawed. Answered in perfect English.

'O Senhor has just asked for four fresh orange juices, and four strong chickens!'

She spluttered: Henry reddened, flustered.

'Is okay. I think that you want four strong coffees, is that correct?'

Henry nodded.

'Then it must be *quatro galões,* Senhor, not *galinhas!*'

'Never mind, Henry, you rock. Three cheers for Henry!' and Stefan led a rousing chorus.

'Be quiet, for goodness sake, you're an embarrassment,' boomed Mum. 'The trouble with you, Henry, is that you just don't pay attention to detail – never have. Would drive me round the bend.' Aha. Here was Mother, Atilla: I was wondering where she'd gone in my honeymoon of bonhomie and romanticism of the last two 'just call me Lena' rose-coloured days.

We sat down: my take was confirmed.

'And sweetheart, what will you wear tonight?' She looked me up and down. 'I mean those shorts are nice, and the flat shoes very comfortable, I'm sure, but you never did have the best ankles, did you, so I hope you're going to wear a little heel, even if it's only a kitten.'

No one looked at each other. I didn't cry. I did fantasize her with a strong chicken where her head should be, and that seemed to help me to keep some control.

'Actually, MOTHER, my legs are fine and my ankles are much trimmer than they used to be. I do those calf raises, you know, they've made a huge difference, so they blend much more into my long slim legs now. Which I must have got from Dad.'

I smiled sweetly amongst a discernible group intake of breath, but I knew that Atilla and I were fine. Back on more familiar territory. Nice that we had had some schmoozing, actually very special.

'Ow, sharp enough to shave your legs with,' I heard Jutta whisper to Tammi, who was just giggling.

We drank our coffee and revelled in the sunshine. I realized I hadn't done any more than slap on some sun cream, and suspected that I might need to unpack the bags which were bound to be lurking under my eyes, so by 11.30 I instigated the return to the villa, where a hog roast was being prepared outside, and space being created for salads and so on. How on earth a dozen of us were going to eat all this I didn't know, but anyway, that particular ball was in Henry's court.

I had a text when I got back, from Jon. 'Happy birthday, Mama, sorry not to be there.'

Short and sweet.

I went and had a long relaxing bath, liberally sprinkled with rose oil, put on a soothing avocado face mask and lush cucumber eye pads. I fed my skin lavishly, and then, before I knew it, wrapped in a thick towel and feeling very mellow, I fell asleep on the bed, verandah doors open, the sounds of the family outside on the patio. I could hear Jutta's voice droning on, something about 'of course it's classic mother-daughter rivalry, I mean Freud missed that with his obsession with women having an absence of penis', and then Stefan, countering, 'Yes, well that's where Melanie Klein was so intelligent, wasn't it, she went much more into the female psyche; I'm surprised women counsellors don't do more to get her into the curriculum, instead of depending on all those men whose theories you teach.'

The last words I heard were Jutta's, 'Well, Stefan, if you don't mind me saying so, that last remark sounds just a little aggressive, a little *I'm okay but you're not*, hey?'

I knew that I was very okay not to be out there in that particular exchange, and smiled to myself.

The next I knew, there was my Henry, waking me gently with a kiss and another tray – this time iced water, melon, goats cheese and honey on thin whole meal toast. What a star.

His stardom slightly paled when he intimated that we might make love, because I was quite clear that there would be no production or abandonment of bodily secretions on my rose oiled skin today, thank you, so I hit that notion straight on the head.

Half of my birthday has already gone then, and we're getting ready for the party. We've arranged champagne cocktails on the patio at 6 p.m., so I'm going to have a good old titivate, and Rosie is going to do my nails for me, and I'm wearing my one pair of Jimmy Choos, as it happens, so I know my ankles will be looking very fab, thank you, and then *va va voom!* I'll be off, kicking and screaming indelicately into my next phase of life.

the auspicious birthday

april 22nd 2010

Madness. Sheer madness. This is the first moment I've had to myself since it happened, and I'm so exhausted I can hardly write. After all my preparations, all my hopes, my careful planning and self-care, I have to say that I feel about seventy-five years old, let alone fifty. And as for mid-life crisis – well, inevitable, really, and I feel like I've just been in a Fool's Paradise the last few weeks.

Maybe even years.

Was it the drink – the air – the family dynamic – who knows. Whatever, come my party, years and years of pent-up energy must have got inside one of the party bags, shaken itself up and exploded all over paradise.

And those poor SAGA people. I just can't imagine how they are.

I am ahead of myself. I have a large gin and tonic here, but despite everything I am determined not to smoke, as I promised myself that I would stop when I'm fifty, and to keep my promises seems to be the only way to restore some kind of order now. As Mother always said – and how differently now I view her than a week ago – there is no such thing as a disaster, only a learning opportunity. So I'm going to take myself back and relive yesterday as if it's happening, for you to get the gist, and me to find the sodding opportunity.

But I'm all over the place, so forgive me if I digress here and there.

You know, an accident scene is nothing like you might expect. On the TV, it's kind of predictable, and contained. You see it approaching, you hear a few sounds, you feel some adrenaline. And then it's over. Camera pans to car, where everyone, whatever state they may be in, is lying quietly.

In reality, it's quite the opposite. For a start, you don't see it coming. You don't. Not if you are standing on the verandah of a holiday villa, overlooking all your friends and relatives partying poolside, music blasting out of a borrowed music system, while the pool man is standing behind you, persistently trying to seduce you, his arms around your waist, his erection pressing into your

148

backside. And you are looking at your husband and suddenly having a blinding flash of the bleeding obvious as he and the other pool man lean toward each other in the pink elephant blow up chair that is in the pool.

I'm ahead again. Order.

We begin the evening with the champagne cocktails on the patio. There we are, just the eight of us, the smell of hog and clay cooked chicken emanating from the back terrace of the house. The catering company are mixing magical spells, Moroccan spices, and I know it's going to be special.

Henry is looking good, dressed in the silk paisley shirt. He is moving, dancing to the music, with the hips of a different man from the one on the plane with his eye pads and earplugs. That man was adept at shutting down his senses. This man, relaxed and loose, is embracing them all. He is charming, making sure we all have our glasses filled, singing along, kissing all the women, on top form.

I'm fifty, special efforts are being made all round, I tell myself.

I breathe in the ambience of the garden. There are scented candles and giant joss sticks positioned everywhere. Before I know it, Connie is surprising me by announcing her new business venture.

'Cloth notepads,' she declares, 'I'm going to develop a range of ecologically sound reuseable notepads that don't cost an arm and a leg, that wash easily, and I'm going to make them a huge success. My friend Nance who I used to go to school with is an expert in e-business, and we're going to do it together. I'm going to call it Earth Note.' She juts out her chin.

I am impressed, if a little surprised.

'Fabulous, Connie, you've got such a good brain. And it's a good business, and will save 10.3% of the national paper wastage just in the UK alone if everyone were to switch to reusable notepads.' Mother's comments are abuzz with accurate detail, a consequence of her quizzing hobby and fine attention to detail.

'What about Michael, didn't he always want you to be a stay at home wife?'

I query her gently.

She replies, not gently.

'Michael can fuck off, quite frankly, and the next time he wants his bloody floors waxed and his dining table laid and entertainment laid on for the Senior Management, he can sodding well do it himself. Up yours, to the lot of them.'

Don't mention the children, I think.

Rosie gets there first.

'It'll be good for Pru and Seb to see that you have a life of your own.'

'D'you know what, Rosie, I sometimes think I wouldn't care if it was good for them or not. All my life I'm trying to get what's good for them, the right cereal, the right after school classes, the right shoes, and Seb is still a little jumped up prick like his father, and Pru will rebel and then settle down with a man, and so good luck to them, I say, but I'm just going to do this for me.'

Stefan, I notice, is passing some canapés to Connie, hoping perhaps that they will soak up some of the champagne, but she isn't having it. I am then distracted by Henry, who is telling me that we have guests to welcome. I don't see Connie after that till much later on, when I remember noticing her doing cartwheels at the side of the pool, registering that I didn't know she could do them.

The guests are Antonia Moanier and Fred.

'Darling.'

Antonia and I kiss the air near each other's cheeks. She is nearly wearing a halter neck number with a split up the back, and she takes earnest hold of my hands as she looks me up and down.

'You know, Izzie, I think I shall make you my role model. How simply fabulous that even after all these children,' – she waves a well-manicured and spectacularly heavily diamonded hand in the general direction of my family – 'you manage to look so wonderful, *for your age*. I hope that when I am in my fifties, although that's a while yet, I will be able to get away with as much as you can.'

Did I grin? I don't know. I do know that as she peppers the seeming sweetness with venom, I let my own newly manicured nails dig deep into her wrists, enough to make her shut up and leave me alone for a while. I hug Fred, and then I open my gifts, chosen by Antonia, carried by Fred.

Two yoga blocks, a skipping rope, and a full set of Esteé Lauder skin repair serums for mature skin. I dispatch Henry to put them safely away, and thank the little cow profusely.

A small trickle of people then turn up: a woman called Suzie who Tammi met on the guided walk, with her son Pedro.

The couple we met in the pub, to my complete surprise, Claudia and Matt – she brings me a little book, *Fifty Turning Fifty*, real live accounts of women turning fifty and surviving – 'to give you hope', Claudia says. Clearly, my last meeting with her when I described my sexual flings with Marc have led her to believe there is little of that particular quality in my life.

And then, Jean. Jean, fatty, salad dodger, happiest face in the world, enters in a flurry of noisy family, those we'd seen at the Beach Bar the previous day. And bless her, she does no more than present me with a huge bottle of Pimms, and a massive box of Thorntons. I love her in that moment, as she kisses me and says, meaning every word, 'Put those away for yourself, a girl can never have too many chocolates, happy birthday, Izzie, let's have a bloody good crack.'

Henry is buttling away, taking my presents to the fridge, and making sure that everyone has drinks, even though there are now waitresses to help to do that.

And then, as music is throbbing, everyone mingling, eating delicious pork, Moroccan chicken, a whole host of lovely things, Joe and Vlad turn up. They are carrying flowers – a whole bunch of orange and purple days eye for me, and a single one flower, deep pink, for Henry.

'For buttonhole.' Vlad smiles, pins the flower on Henry's chest. Kisses me, quickly, just as I am questioning something about Henry in my mind again. I decide it can all wait until tomorrow.

So we are officially partying, more like a loosely arranged dinner event in motion, but lovely, the dimming day heralding another wonderful starry night and big moon, everyone mellow, me very excited, very happy. Jutta chatting up Vlad, Tammi with Suzie, Stefan and Rosie spending time together, Mother buttonholing Fred – everything just flowing for a good couple of hours or so.

Until I go upstairs. Quickly followed by Joe, and as soon as we are alone, we kiss, passionately, deeply, me feeling more alive than for years. Giggling, feeling the years shed, loving it, seeing everyone being happy, and then telling Joe to calm down. The night is yet young, and I take him out on the verandah to survey my celebration.

The music is *Pink Martini*, very suave, very Latino, and people are dancing around. I am noticing Henry in the blow up chair in the pool, the large pink elephant chair that Vlad has brought for the celebrations. Jutta is in the other chair, floating near, watching them, looking slightly put out. Henry and Vlad have their arms around each other. They are so drunk, shouting out 'bottoms up', slurping champagne from plastic cups, turning and presenting their bottoms up literally. They fall in the pool, and when they clamber out, hysterical and holding each other up, they take it upon themselves to drag the pink blow up elephant chair out of the pool as well. They whoop it up in the air and the next thing I see is that the chair is caught by a gust of Algarvian wind and is flying over the garden wall right out onto the road beyond.

No, you don't see an accident coming. You hear it. The terrible screeching of tyres, the high-pitched squealing of brakes, the useless, desperate blast of a horn. Then you smell it, burning rubber and perhaps a hint of your own fear, and just as you realize that something might be wrong, there is an almighty crashing bang and the first screams become audible.

Only then do you see that an accident was about to happen.

As the vehicle continues to bounce and screech, and even when it comes to a stop, the sounds are phenomenal. The screaming goes on, and people in the garden begin to realize that something is very wrong, and they unite in a deep silence punctuated only by 'what the fuck...?', and 'oh my God', and Stefan turns the music off, and there is groaning, and there is scrunching and squealing, the noise of body parts rearranging themselves and bits of metal settling precariously into different positions.

And then a second crunch, because something must have ploughed into the first vehicle.

And the first vehicle must have been coming around the bend at precisely the moment when the blow up chair was falling from the sky. God knows what the driver, who we now know as Mr Ribeiro, must have thought as he found himself in the surreal situation of driving through a typical Algarvian night, stars shining down from the curved ceiling of the world, when he sees a pink elephant flying towards him. Its lightweight reality probably escaped him, and he swerved to avoid it.

Straight into the wall.

With his precious cargo of a party of seven, courtesy of SAGA holidays, tightly packed into his minibus. With his wife, who is along for the ride.

The accident was the most shocking experience that I have ever had. But I must tell you, what happened next was the most *surprising*. Fred, bless him, wasted no time, he jumped the wall and was down the drive in a split second it seemed. Jutta was out of the pool, shouting, 'I'm phoning for an ambulance I'm phoning for an ambulance.' Joe climbed over the balcony and jumped down from the roof below, and in seconds was running down the drive as well. I realised that I'd been shocked into stillness a good ten or twenty seconds, and I shook myself and ran downstairs to go and join the others. I took the situation in quickly, then. The driver got out of the car and as I arrived I saw him collapsing into someone's arms. He was muttering words which sounded like 'more air, more air', which I realised later was actually *minha mulher* – my wife. I could see that next to the driver's seat was a woman, her head hanging down. Joe was talking to her in an urgent voice speaking Portuguese, a *dona*, something or another, and Vlad was now by his side, saying 'let me, I know First Aid, let me.'

I ran to the back and to my surprise saw that Rosie was there already. A woman was screaming and crying, screaming words that I didn't understand. I saw that Rosie was with a man who had blood running all down his head, and as she helped him out of the car, he vomited, projectile vomiting all over her front. Rosy didn't flinch, just took him to her and wiped his face with her skirt. The woman looked at Rosy pleadingly, and Rosie was saying, 'It's alright it's all right, the vomit doesn't matter.' She caught my eye. I went to the mother. She had slid from her seat so that she was squashed up in the space between back seat and front seat. I could smell shit.

I could see blood pouring from a wound somewhere on the woman, I didn't know where, but I was wary of moving her. I could smell petrol, and didn't know how dangerous that might be. I summoned all my strength and found myself trying to breathe out deeply and calmly as if I could somehow influence things. 'Here', I said, 'let me' and I put my arms out to the woman, who shook her head at first, screeching almost hysterically. Suddenly I heard a man's voice soft gentle speaking to her, while I stroked her face. I realised it was Joe's voice, asking her where it hurt, telling her that we needed to move her if we possible could, checking she could

153

feel and move all of her limbs, what did she think. He coaxed her out, and helped me to take her inside, carrying her between us on a fireman's chair. Once we were in better light I could see that the woman was very pale but seemingly not badly hurt. Connie greeted us, she had found a pile of clean towels and had beside her two bowls of water. She had a sheet which she had torn into pieces. Connie gently wiped the woman's face, and we wrapped her shoulders in a warm fluffy towel. Then I held her to me, and to my surprise, Connie put a blanket around my shoulders and said, 'Well done, Mum.' Suddenly, I burst into tears, crying and rocking this woman just like I used to rock Connie all those years ago. Connie put her arms around me and said, 'I know, Mum, I know', and kissed me on my cheek before going to help someone else.

It's a bit blurry then, the woman and I stopped crying, and I sat her down and poured her a little *maciera*, and she was calm by the time the ambulance arrived. I can only remember little cameos around the place: Rosie with the man, him laid on a sofa and her softly talking to him and cleaning him; Connie buzzing around, making space, conjuring these rags and towels and even cups of tea, and spoonfuls of sugar, and goodness knows what. It wouldn't have surprised me if she hadn't waxed a floor or two: I saw Tammi with Henry, who looked totally confused and red-eyed, and she was talking to him; I didn't see Vlad, but discovered that together with Joe, he had rescued the older woman, the driver's wife, out of the car, and carried her up the drive. I saw her in Jutta's care, she had put her in the recovery position and wrapped her in blankets and then focused on doing Reiki since the old lady looked unconscious.

Absolute heroes.

I heard mother, supervising. 'Don't move her too much in case of broken bones, put that one in the recovery position, oh look, he's faint, head between his knees now.'

And Henry was still crying, red-eyed, into Tammi's boundless unconditional space of friendship.

I think we waited about twenty-five minutes for the police and two ambulances to arrive. By then, Mrs Ribeiro had come around, and was drinking hot sweet tea and Rosie and I were beside her. Everyone looked battered and bruised, but I couldn't see more than that. We knew it had been risky to move them from the car, but the guys were worried that it would catch fire because of the leaking petrol. It didn't in fact, although the fire brigade came as well. Shortly after, a few people arrived from the village, obviously they had heard the commotion. One of them, a short dark woman called Irena came to me and kissed me on both cheeks. 'You save their life, kind lady', and cried effusively all over the place. My body was racked with guilt, yet touched by how kind everyone was being, which just kind of made it worse.

Amazingly, in the end, none of the injuries were too bad. Mr Ribeiro was the worst off – he had a punctured lung, and a broken ankle, as well as some cuts and bruising to his face. Mrs Ribeiro had two fractured ribs, and the others all escaped with cuts and bruises. It turned out that Mr Ribeiro had been drinking heavily, which bizarrely then made me feel better, maybe it wasn't all our fault.

And he shouldn't have had his wife with him, strictly speaking, not on minicab duty.

And then, the strangest thing. One of the last passengers to get fully into the house was almost smiling, probably one of the younger SAGA people, maybe in her sixties, and had a touch of white powder around her nose which intrigued me.

'Where's that lovely young man?' she said, and at first I thought she meant Joe, but it appeared that some alternative medical therapist had been passenger in a taxi that had then run into the minibus, and had been dishing out some kind of powder for them which he told them was a rescue remedy.

And just as I was putting this information together, and victims were slowly being transported off into ambulances and police cars, I saw the young man in question come to the patio doors, and I caught his eye.

His very slightly dilated eye.

'Hello, Mum, happy birthday.' Jon was grinning and looking like he hadn't got a care in the world.

I think that's all I can say for now. By the time the ambulances had gone, the staff from the Beach Bar had come and joined us, and we now had quite a full house, so, as we all talked about what had happened, the music went back on and the drinks came round again – and again – and we partied.

I have to go now, to talk to Henry, because some quite strange things are going on, and to Jon, who was the biggest surprise of the night, and assess where I am.

Or rather, what the fuck is going on.

confessions of an old married couple

april 23rd 2010

So, I still have things to tell you from the last two days, but as usual the future has arrived and become the present, and I can hardly believe it but both Rosie and Stefan had to go today. Stefan to get back for his last exam, and Rosie, my dear Rosie, has been here for a week already. I have barely even thought about a face mask or a cucumber eye patch, although now is probably the precise time when I should be paying attention to these details, especially since yes, I did have sex with Joe, pure, unadulterated, animal sex, in touch with the preciousness of each minute, each hour, of this life.

We partied, as I said, and around us the caterers quietly did their clearing up and Stefan DJ'ed admirably, something for everyone. Mother, I noticed, had Fred doing a tango at one point, both of them laughing uproariously while Antonia Moanier draped herself over a chair, flirting with Suzie's son in a desperate kind of way – I mean, seventeen, no compliment there if she managed to raise any interest, at that age a lad would fuck a pikelet, as one of my ex-lovers used to say, so even funnier that she seemingly didn't seem to be getting very far. I couldn't resist a brief remark as I passed.

'I don't know, Antonia,' I smiled, 'where do these older women get their zest? Your Fred looks happy as a pig in shit. Great, isn't it?'

She grimaced at me, giving me attention just long enough for the lad to extricate himself from her clutches. I moved on.

Henry, clearly exhausted by his crying fit, which had not shown him in the best light, sadly useless in fact, had crashed out on a sunlounger. Vlad sat in a chair nearby. Jutta, bless her insensitive and guileless soul, sat next to him, holding his hand.

'Vlad, you must tell me your feelings. These crises are difficult, and in my experience it helps to talk about them soon after they have happened. You must tell me your feelings.'

'My feelings, they are very deep.' Vlad marked his chest with his fist, to show just how deep. 'Is not first time this has

156

happened to me, but this time is very deep. I am – how do you say it – I am knocked over by what has happened here for me.'

Jutta inched closer.

'Oh Vlad, you poor love. You mean you have been involved in an accident like this before?'

Vlad looked puzzled.

I left them to it.

Connie seemed to be spending a lot of time with Jean and her family, and Jon was with them. They shrieked with laughter, and just seemed to be having the best time,

'Good old Charlie! Three cheers to Charlie!' I had no idea what she was on about, but Connie was certainly having a good time.

Now, of course, it's obvious.

And Joe, he mixed with the people from the village, who sat with beers and wine, the women occasionally dancing, the younger men joining them as the night passed, the older ones drifting off as they wanted to, everyone on some sort of adrenaline high.

By about half past five, just before dawn, I found Joe in the kitchen.

'You okay?' he asked me, pushing a strand of hair from my eyes. I rested my head on his shoulder.

'Think so,' I said, 'wow, what a night.'

'Tell you what, Izzie,' he said, 'let's go down to the beach.'

And so we did, we slipped away, and walked down to the beach, and walked along it, the last of the moonlight silver on the calm sea, a hint of the day to come casting pink light over the horizon. We made love there, right there, his body just as warm and strong as I knew it would be, mine just as compliant as I wanted, fitting each other perfectly, moving in rhythm. I don't know if we were noisy or not, but I do know we were passionate.

Seeing an old Portuguese fisherman standing about thirty metres away when we'd done was a bit of a shock, but I just rearranged my clothes, laughed and shouted.

'*Bom dia*, first fuck of my fiftieth year, cheers!'

I thanked my lucky stars that he wouldn't have a clue what I was saying, and thanked my lucky stars that Henry hadn't been there to hear those words.

Henry. Sometime later in the day, when all the sand was washed from my tingling skin – and doesn't it just get everywhere – I found Henry, red-eyed still, and pale. I walked up to him and put my arms around him. He felt awkward, unsure of his body in his own skin.

'It's alright,' I said.

'But I'm not sure it is, Izzie. Something weird has happened. I need to tell you.'

'I know,' I told him, 'It's you and Vlad, I know, and *I* have to tell *you* that it's me and Joe.'

Henry was flabbergasted. I felt calm, unravelling all those clues of the last three weeks, which had crescendoed over this weekend, and the irony of Henry having no idea at all of me and Joe because he was in his own little labyrinth.

We talked then, to the point where we were laughing at ourselves. We wondered about the pool man connection. Could we open a new company, Pool Man Relief Inc., or whatever you would call it over here in Portugal. We ate sandwiches of cold delicious chicken, and cracked a bottle of chilled white, upstairs on our verandah, like two old friends who'd gone a little crazy in the midday sun.

I have no idea what we are going to do about anything, but somewhere in my sleep deprived brain I remembered all that stuff I'd got from Fenella about knowing what you want before deciding what you want to do, and told Henry it didn't matter, yet, we could take our time. In a way it was a huge relief, our lives had become that touch too petty for people like us.

It's all very scary, too, but we've both been around the block a few times. It's not like fear is a new emotion for either of us. Its jaws seem blunter these days to me, its power shrunken.

What's a little fear between life stages, hey?

I couldn't see Jon anywhere, seems he had found the energy to go down to the village, so I showered and allowed exhaustion to wash over me. I lay down in bed, next to my tired old husband, and we wept a little, chuckled a little and then held hands. I think I'm somewhere between numb and hysterical just now, holding hands felt good. I dropped into the deepest sleep.

I woke in the early hours of the day. I got up and went and swam. Then I remembered about Rosie and Stefan. So I dressed and took breakfast provisions round to the house next door where the bougainvillea grows thick and beautiful. They were each in their separate bedrooms, my two babies. I stood in each door way in turn, watching. Stefan's mouth was open, his cheeks pink, still not quite a man yet, having such a great life. Rosie looked serene, and I remembered her calmness in the accident. Whatever her demons had been, I was quite sure they were exorcised. I didn't know yet if we would talk more about Ken, and had managed to observe the silence she had demanded, so far, but there was one thing I wanted to do just to nudge it a little.

I sat outside until they woke, and then made the breakfast up while they rose from their beds, washed, showered, whatever they needed to do. When they were out with me on their terrace, wrapped in light dressing gowns, and drinking the orange juice and coffee, dipping chocolate croissants, I took Ken's bracelet that he had sent me and put it on the table.

'Beautiful, isn't it?' Rosie looked at me, curiosity shining in her eyes.

'Wow.' Stefan nodded.

'Well yes, the object itself is beautiful on its outside, seductively so. And it promises a sense of richness. But I'm going to send it back. It's a bit showy, a bit too good to be true, and I'm sure that if we scratched the surface, we might find the stones a little self-important. I feel it will be too heavy on my wrist, and cause harm to the most sensitive parts. And I would regret forever that I had allowed that to happen, so I will be sending it back to say that to its sender, no more, but to say it very clearly. This is not an appropriate thing to have done, to send this to me, not appropriate at all. I am truly sorry that it ever happened.'

Obviously, Stefan thought I was crazy.

'From Ken? Now what would Melanie Klein say about that, Ma?'

Rosie just took my hand and kissed it.

'You do what you think, Mum, you do what you need.' She paused. 'You know, I'm loving my work with the children, but I'm wondering whether I might at some point look at being a doctor. Something really tangible, you know, where you could make such a difference, healing people, and still keep all that other stuff in your repertoire.

So we chatted, this and that, future careers, two very bright young people, all their lives ahead.

Henry took them to the airport. I was still shattered, and I couldn't do the goodbyes in public, not this time. He was only too pleased, something he could do to be useful, so they went off late morning, and I felt like the reconfiguration of my new world had at least one or two molecules now falling into place.

I will see Joe again soon. And I will catch up with Jon, and spend a little time with Mother and with my lovely girl friends. But for now, I'll just rest.

picnic surprise

april 25th 2010

Got up late this morning, and joined Tammi, Jutta, Mother and Connie on the patio. No sign of Jon. No sign of Henry.

And no more contact with Joe yet – we hadn't got each other's mobile numbers, hadn't thought to swap. He's been a bit of an in the moment thing for me so far.

Now, however, I crave contact. But I need to put everyone into compartments, to be able to cope. All very strange. Now that I know they're a little south of Seville, I have put Henry and Vlad into the compartment to be sorted when everyone has gone. Joe into another box, though if I could get a quick session in with him sometime soon, that could be an exception.

And anyway, it would be doing everyone a favour really, because when you're carrying all that pent-up sexual energy around, you can't think straight, can you.

Attila was surrounded by brain exercising puzzles, while texting away quite frequently, and when she saw me looking, she let me know that it was her new man from the oil rigs, with a somewhat superior grin attached to this imparting of news.

Then went back to her crossword.

'Bugger.'

She looked up sharply, picked up a rubber, erased with passion.

She tutted.

'No wonder I couldn't get that clue. I did it again. I've written "carpe deum" instead of "carpe diem" for 8 Across.'

She looked at me.

'God is a fish,' we said together, entwined our little fingers in recognition of our unity, made a wish, and laughed.

Jon and I decided to go for a walk, which we elaborated by packing a picnic. Long time since I've done that, but in the time when he and Connie were young, we did it a lot, low cost, good fun times in the open air. Okay, so now he's nearly thirty, but hey, we could still do a picnic.

We left Mother and Connie solving more clues. I hadn't realised before that Mother was going slightly deaf. The following conversation alerted me.

Mother: I think I have the answer to this clue, but I'm not quite sure I know what a 'pyrus' is.

Connie: (having rapidly thumbed the keypad of her i-phone) 'Pyrus' is a pear, Nan.

Mother: That pyrus can't be fire, darling, it simply doesn't fit.

Connie: No, Nan, the fruit, pear.

Mother: You mean pair, p - a - i - r?

Connie: No, Lena, pear, p - e - a - r.

Jutta, lazily: That must be where papyrus comes from.

Mother: Paper?

Connie: No, Nan. Pear. P-e-a-r.

Mother: Oh. It's a fruit then.

I suspect that pyrus was not the only fruit present in this exchange.

We set out over the fields Jon and I, to find them peppered with families of swarthy Portuguese, peasant looking Portuguese, rummaging in the long grass. I didn't get what was going on at first, but it turned out they were snail picking, men in various life stages, women with children at their skirts, the children chasing butterflies and carrying buckets, one child running up with their hands out, saying 'money, money'. It seemed a simple kind of life, hard working, resourceful. So far away from our obsessions with psychology, development, wrinkles.

Wrinkles. No, I'd have to draw a line there, mind, because I wouldn't want to have skin like some of those people, more reminiscent of a crumpled paper bag than anything else, so no. I guess simplicity may look a romantic option, but always a price to be paid.

Then again, if I didn't have the awareness of psychology and self-development, then maybe I'd never care about being likened to a paper bag.

Anyway, we were out on the cliff top walk within twenty minutes, the heat rising, the sea doing its magic, tiny dot stuff. We chatted fairly amiably, Jon updating me on his work. Seems he is forever flying hither and thither, jet-setting stuff, high profile exec, loving it. We found a spot to sit, lightly shaded, just off the main path, and laid down our cloth and our wares from the cool bag –

white wine, water, light chicken sandwiches with mayo, on brown, of course, and some strawberries.

'And socially, Jon, what do you do socially? Lots of partying?'

Yes, of course he did, no one special person in his life, lots of great times.

'And the coke, Jon, is that recreational, or is that what gets you through this lifestyle of yours?'

I think I surprised him, but I hadn't just fallen off a Christmas tree, and somewhere in my recall of my party the reference to Charlie had suddenly made sense, and I knew it was one of the whites or browns that he was using, because of the eyes. I had thought it might be speed, but now it all fell into place and I could see that my hunch was right by Jon's reaction.

Don't get me wrong, I'm no moralist on recreational drug use, but I'm very practical and know the difference between a bit of a dabble and a dependency. A dependency is never good, always curbs your freedom, and often brings real downers alongside the highs. I didn't want that for my son. My bright, sensitive son.

'Aha,' he said to me, 'you know. I was crazy to think you wouldn't, of course. It's just crept up on me, Mum, you know, a bit here, a bit there, to keep me going.'

I nodded. Yes, I did know, actually, quite well. I just for some reason always manage to pull out of my excesses at the eleventh hour.

Apart from those that involved me getting pregnant, that is.

'And the bugger of it is, I get so bloody well paid, I can afford it. Or I could, at any rate.' He downed a swig of white wine (legal drug, so that was okay), and looked way over the horizon.

Then he turned to me.

'But to be honest, it's got a bit on top of me lately. It's not great. I've been looking at going into rehab.'

Oh.

'Because?'

'It's all wrong, Mum, work's wrong, the parties are boring, without getting out of my skull, and I'm not really sure I want to be out of it anymore.'

Oh lord. My whole family, stealing my thunder. This should be *my* mid-life crisis, instead of which Connie is giving up domestic bliss for recyclable notebooks and doing cartwheels down the poolside, and I'm sure I'm right when I recall that she too was toasting dear old Charlie the other night? Rosie had been laying ghosts to rest, Mother running off with a bit of rough from the oil rigs, Henry coming out (almost, he seems to have gone a bit in somewhere just now, but I'm sure he'll resurface) and now Jon.

My family, all fur coats and no knickers.

I love them to bits.

Made my shagging the pool man look pretty minor.

I must have smiled.

'It's not funny, Mum.'

'No, well no, it's not. But aren't you brilliant, Jon, to want to get it sorted.'

I took his face in my hands, and kissed him, hugged him.

'Does your father know about it?'

We had a good chat then, and actually moved through loads of subjects, before Jon dropped the last little bombshell.

'Anyway, part of my stay in Lahore was to wrap up some business there so that I could be free for rehab. And as it happens, Mum, one of the best rehab units I've been recommended is right here in the Algarve. I'm going to have a look tomorrow on the way to the airport. It's between that and the one in South Africa. Either way, I'm not staying in London.'

I asked him to let me know how it goes.

So tonight it's a farewell meal for everyone. Suzie is coming too, my dear Tammi complicating her life as ever, and we're going to a restaurant that has a fab reputation and apparently ends the meals by giving us huge glasses of brandy or port to share, so I guess it will be a late one.

Bring it on.

through the looking glass

april 26th 2010

So off we went, to the *O Celeiro* restaurant, where we were greeted by hunky great waiters who seated us and then came brandishing fresh fish on platters, and steaks and goodness knows what to choose from.

The head waiter twinkled at Tammi and Suzie, who were fanning each other's flames with the subtlety of a brick, more heat sizzling around them than the steaks on a stone on the next table. He smiled and raised an eyebrow.

'And for our Sapphic sisters?' He proffered the fish.

Henry was full of booze and bonhomie, sitting next to Tammi, and insisted on buying us all champagne to begin with.

Jutta sat next to me, and within minutes she was speaking to me *voce sotto*.

'You know, Izzie, I'm a little bit worried about you.'

I took a burning sausage from the range of *couverts* that had appeared on the table, a rich array of bread, olives, carrots, cheeses, meats, and nibbled it.

'I mean, great party and so on, but so much has happened and you have all that guilt to deal with about the accident, and then Joe, and now what about Henry? I mean, he looks in a right state.'

I blinked at her. I wasn't really sure what she knew in detail, what she didn't. I resolved that in future I would only have one friend over at a time. There they all were, yet I seemed in a bubble far away.

'I think he'll be fine, Jutta, and no, I don't really feel guilty about Saturday. It's a bit surreal, I have to say, and I did wonder if I should go hospital visiting. But I'm over it.'

Henry joined in.

'I'm going to the police station tomorrow, the GNR,' he announced. 'Vlad's going to come with me to translate. Just to take in all our paperwork.'

He slurped from the bubbly fountain in front of him.

'There, perfect,' I said, 'Henry's got it all under control.'

I raised my glass.

Jutta hissed.

'For goodness sake, Izzie, does he look like a man who's got anything under control? I mean, open your eyes for goodness sake.'

She too was imbibing the bubbly nectar.

I took a pickled carrot from the tray, sucked it.

'How about you, Jutta?' I said. 'Were you a bit disappointed about Vlad?'

She reddened, just a touch.

'No,' she said. 'He wasn't quite my cup of tea. Actually, I think I might join an internet relationship coaching site. I don't think I want to bother with the sex side, I may be too old.'

The memory of Jutta's thronged arse slipped, unwelcome, into my memory. I shooed it out, quickly.

We chatted away, and she took wine, ended up turning to Henry and having a good blart on his shoulder, and in the end we were playing games, 'if you were a celebrity who would you be and why'. There were no surprises, Jon wanted to be David Bowie, a bit retro but no surprise since he is my son☺, Connie wanted to be Linda McCartney (the alive version), Tammi and Suzie wanted to be Sarah Waters and Dusty Springfield, respectively, Henry fancied being Graham Norton, Jutta wanted to be Oprah, and me, I wanted to be Debbie Harry.

'Great game,' I said to Jutta, 'a lot faster and cheaper than all that counselling and psychotherapy, cuts right to the chase.'

And that was it really, nothing of significance to report, just a merry evening drinking and eating, avoiding any mention or addressing of the cataclysmic experience that was going on beneath mine and Henry's feet, and we ended by drinking port from the longest glass in the world, and drinking brandy from brandy glasses so big that you could get your whole head into it, and that was that. Tearful and loving nigh-nights before everyone was to leave.

I wonder if I *should* worry about Henry?

raging fires within

april 27th 2010

But that was last night, and so much has happened today, yet nothing really in my head except for Joe. He came to do the pool. Everyone was packing up to go, and to be honest, I left them to it for most of the day. They're all grown up. I'm slightly tiring of the company now and anyway, my whole life seemed to be beating in the space between navel and groin. Home of the big red chakra.

In other words, I was feeling randy as hell.

Yes, so he did the pool and then came over to have a quiet word. He wanted to meet me later, had somewhere to show me. So I set it up that I would walk down to the beach around 5 p.m. which I did.

We had to be a bit careful. It was exciting, remembering the last time I was there with him, all that sand in my knickers, all that passion. But Joe lived here, I didn't really know what level of village knowledge or gossip he'd be happy with, or not. My large Gucci's were really welcome, gave me a little cover. We kissed, of course, orthodox, just a tiny bit of tongue mingling as we were in transit between cheeks, and he murmured something to me.

Anyway, once all this was done, and we inflamed each other's secret desires, he took my elbow, like a nice young man helping out a tourist, or a client.

'Come with me, Izzie, I want to take you to meet my uncle.'

I had no idea that Joe had an uncle here, and said so.

'He was one of the ones on the SAGA bus,' said Joe, and I groaned inwardly wondering what damage we might have done the poor old bugger. Joe gave me a funny smile, and insisted that we go despite my protestations. He took me up some steps from the beach, into a little maze of tiny back alleys, sardines cooking here and there on tiny barbecue trays outside open doors, cats slinking round the smelly fish cobbles, sun twinkling off windows edged with blue. When we got to the house he wanted, Joe pushed past the beaded curtain hanging in the door way, and we went into a dark cool room crowded with what seemed like far too many chairs, wherein sat a woman and a man, the man with his legs up on a footstool.

Not the usual holiday villa.

'Tee-oo.' Joe bent and shook the man's hand, said something in Portuguese that I didn't understand. Then pulled me across.

'This is my uncle, Izzie, Senhor Ribeiro.'

'Jorge.'

The man smiled, a gap-toothed smile gashing weather wrinkled skin, and as I bent to greet him I saw bruises and realized that this was he, the driver from the SAGA holiday bus, the man with the punctured lungs.

He who had lived the day when pink elephants could fly.

I must have gasped, because Joe laughed and said, 'It's okay, Izzie, he's fine, and he doesn't blame you. Accidents happen, and he had taken a touch more port than he should have done, so don't worry.'

The woman got up and kissed both of my cheeks, then kissed and gabbled on to Joe, before going into the kitchen to make some tea. Mr Ribeiro winked at Joe, and reached purposefully down the side of his chair, whence he pulled up a large white wicker flask, motioning to Joe to get cups, and before we knew it we were drinking red wine that tasted like it might be harbouring a real mule kick.

Turned out that Joe's dad was Portuguese. His mum had only come on holiday here however many years ago and fallen in love with a Portuguese fisher man, Jorge's younger brother. They'd moved eventually to England, though his dad had never settled there, so his dad had come back here, but had died some time ago, drowned. Joe came out here every year, and this time he was staying for a while.

Mrs Ribeiro, Teresa, came back in with a tray laden with *pasteis de natas*, custard tart type cakes, and an almond cake. And a big sloppy flan ring, which turned out to be called *pudim flan*, like a very light crème caramel. I tried everything, and nobody talked about weight, or fat, or what you should or shouldn't eat, and Joe translated between us while we exchanged pleasantries, and then when Teresa told me that I must come to dinner one night. She touched Joe's shoulder and told me he was 'very good boy'. I thought her immensely liberal, to accept me just like that, a woman of my age, being with her young nephew, and said so to Joe.

'What did you tell her?'

He grinned again.

'She thinks that I'm your servant,' he said, 'cleaning your pool and now helping you find your way around the village for some shopping.'

Hilarious. My servant. Yes, I could go for that, and had plenty of things on my list that he could do for me.

I wondered if Teresa would be smiling so affably if she could read my mind.

Jorge wondered whether we'd seen any of the old people off the bus, and wanted to know why the English sent their old people away on a holiday all together, instead of going with their families? In Portugal, he told Joe to tell me, the family would always look after the old people, and they would all travel together to the north in the summer, taking the grandchildren with a bucket of fish and homemade cakes.

We left after half an hour or so, and snaked our way up the cliff tops overlooking the beach. We chatted, and I told Joe that while this was fun, I was very confused now about what had happened between us and needed time to think, and that we needed to shelve our obvious lust for each other. I had a lot to work out, so best just stay platonic for now.

Joe agreed, and then when we were far enough away from the village to know that we were totally secluded, he grabbed me and I succumbed and we made love in a frenzied half-dressed kind of way, once again the passion rising in me like I hadn't known for ages before Joe. When we were spent, we walked back to the road and over the back hills, where Joe left me to make my way home on my own.

Henry was waiting for me, looking red-eyed and red-wined again, and once I'd showered, I sat with him on the terrace.

'We need to talk,' he said,' shall we go out tonight?'

I agreed, yes, we would, and so that's what we're going to do. I've no idea what we're really going to talk about, though I know that the list is endless of what we should talk about. Tammi has texted, 'safely home, a right old tangle, fabulous to see you, great start to the next half century'.

I suppose that's one way to put it.

roles and responsibilities

april 28th 2010

So, we went, Henry and I, back to Salema, where we'd had such a lovely lunch way back before we had been taken over by lust and rapaciousness, before a truckload of the elderly and vulnerable had crashed into the garden wall.

I let him know that Jon changed his plans after we had our picnic, and didn't even bother going back to London at all. He's booked himself in and tootled off to the recovery centre, *Segunda Vida* which literally means Second Life. It's in the foothills of the mountains. He's texted and warned me that he won't be in contact for some time, no phones allowed, no music, no internet access. Apparently, that makes it easier for the addicts to be tempted into old ways, although for the life of me I can't see how he'd get a line of coke hidden in a mobile phone. And perhaps a bit of relaxation music might be just the ticket. Still, I suppose they know what they're doing.

Henry made the right supportive noises, said that I seemed to be taking it calmly.

'But what about us?'

Once I focused on the inevitability of this question, I felt really wary, guilty, at how I'd let Henry down. I hoped we could talk gently.

We ordered Martinis, sat out on the verandah, which felt deliciously private.

After the first, very large, gulp, so large that we virtually emptied our glasses in one, I took Henry's hand.

'I'm so sorry, Henry, I just don't know where to start.'

He looked at me, slightly uncomprehending.

'For what? Why are you sorry?'

The waiter came across with bread rolls, sardine pâté, olives, carrots, and raised an eyebrow.

'More drinks?'

'Yes, large ones, *f-faz favor*.'

Dear Henry, so persistent, so trying. Alcohol definitely seemed to be his new crutch.

Thank heavens.

He watched the waiter walk away.

'He is so-o callipygian,' he ventured, 'don't you think?'

I know it sounds ridiculous, but it surprised me when I realised that Henry was not commenting objectively, in his irritating Latin prep school way, about the shapely buttocks of our waiter, but was actively lusting after him And somewhat belatedly, now that I put it all together, the full blown truth finally hit me.

Henry really is gay. He wasn't just having a drunken skirmish, a transient behavioural attack while under the influence. He really was – is – fully-fledged gay.

And I had been so careful and concerned our first two weeks or so, lest I hurt him by making love with a perfectly understandably desirable young man, and in fact being very noble about it until after the party, which I hadn't had to be: and now I wondered about the fishing trip, Henry and Vlad. perhaps it had been more than a stray sardine that Vlad had hooked that day on the end of his rod.

Suddenly I wasn't so sorry.

'So, how long have you known?' I asked him, swigging rather than sipping the Martini, chomping rather than nibbling at the mint garnish, taking a knife to the sardine pâté tin.

He flushed.

'It's hard to say. I suppose for a long time. But I can go either way.'

I thought back to the dropping of the golf trews, to many an occasion, in fact, when we'd had passionate sex and yet where I, for one, had been in fantasy land, and not fully sated. Had it been like that for Henry? Is sexual union, in the end, just a matter of bodily convenience? Are the sensuality of touch and the presence of friction simply mechanical necessities, the real essence of sexuality residing in the brain?

'Jeffrey Weeks was right then.'

The name popped up from somewhere in the recesses of my mental filing cabinet, the social construction of sexuality and all that.

'So how long is a long time?'

'School, I suppose.'

The space between us hovered, expectant.

'But I kind of knew and didn't know. As if my inclinations compacted like an iceberg, I could see the tip but the rest – the rest, Izzie, was concealed.'

171

He reached a hand out into the taut air between us.

I kept mine to myself.

'Even from me.'

I pondered, swigged, feasted on the pâté and bread, sucked an olive and spat out the stone. I decided there was nothing more to ask there, that particular part of Henry's life was, and must stay, his own. It just was as it was.

Except for one question.

'And if you can go either way, tell me, Henry, which do you prefer?'

I noticed a head turn on the table just inside the door, sporting a raised eyebrow. I glared, so that its owner swivelled quickly back to their own business.

Henry lifted his glass at the same time as I, and I returned the energy of my focus to him, daring him to try and slip out of this one.

'It's not like that.' He almost whispered.

'But if you had to choose, go on, absolutely had to?' Intrigue and frustration fuelled me.

'I can't.'

'So just now. Which is most exciting, Vlad or me?'

I was sure I heard the creak of that nosey turning head again, but by now I couldn't care less who could hear us.

He looked sad, then, Henry, like a caged animal. I felt like a predator. Throughout the last couple of weeks of flirting with Joe, I'd resisted and hated the tag cougar for older women who get off with younger men. But now, here in this restaurant, I felt like a big cat, waiting to pounce.

So that when he said, gently, about Vlad being exciting because he was f-f-forbidden f-f-fruit, I had a f-field day. Tears with the avocado starter, and green wine. Dramatic outrage with the swordfish and the white Alentejo wine, *how could you do this to me?* And then, by the *tarte da nata* stage, and the sweet Madeira wine, a sense of hysteria.

So that we laughed. Laughed until we cried, the space between us relaxing, bridged by shared emotions, then with great hugs and kisses, Henry saying that this was just a holiday romance and he couldn't possibly pursue it. He needed time to work things out, to maybe have a bit of counselling, or support, or whatever it is that people do when the iceberg of their hidden sexual preference begins to melt and make waves in the ocean.

'James would have a fit.'

I could see it now, Henry going back to the UK, Director of the company, his Russian pool cleaner partner in tow. My vision appealed. I pledged Henry my undying support and loving friendship, and we were sure it would all work out, because after all we're very mature, and would I really want Henry *not* to be happy? I don't think so.

We poured ourselves into a taxi back to our village, and emptied ourselves into the pub, for *maciera* and coffee. I have a theory that if you have a coffee with every *maciera*, you don't get drunk.

But it is only a theory.

The Scissor Sisters were on just as we walked in, so before we knew it, Henry and I were dancing round that old pole, a pair of self-deluded gazelles who probably looked more like hippos to the untrained eye, but what the heck.

Don't remember much more, we saw one or two familiar faces, and clearly we got home safely, because here I am.

The coffee didn't work. The ibuprofen is beginning to.

And now just one more thing to deal with before tomorrow, and that is Joe. Who didn't come up at all in our conversation last night, so convinced was I that I was a victim of duplicity and treachery.

Funny, isn't it, how you can kid yourself to almost believe your own lies?

But deal with him I must, because I'll be going home very soon and I can't do that without saying goodbye.

parting is such sweet sorrow

april 29th 2010

My holiday is almost over.

I read back through this blog and I feel confused. My face, the subject of such care and attention in the early days, is like a lilo, bloated and pillowy. My eyes are red, and my skin is dry. The Clarins hasn't even been out this week, that's how bad it is. I am fifty years old, and I've had a crazy month.

I saw Joe. We met on the beach, and I felt first of all as if in a dream, removed. From the distance I created, I saw a young man, younger than my detoxifying son, a young man with an interesting, maybe complicated past. Savvy beyond years, vulnerable with youth. I saw a predator, maybe still having a bit of a laugh at my expense, someone who cleaned pools and met hundreds of women, some of them lonely and a tiny bit empty.

I didn't really believe that second take. Really, he is just a young man of some discernment☺.

I could see me. Women can always see themselves from the outside in, whereas men are more likely to be looking from the inside out. I think John Berger said that. I saw a middle-aged woman, someone who'd had chance after chance, so lucky in the richness of her family and friends, desperately fighting off the signs of ageing, grasping at straws. I saw a middle-aged woman being exactly that, middle-aged, loads of time to go yet with an appreciation of living life to the full, because she knows it won't last forever.

Once my philosophising was over, and I climbed down from my ethereal cloud, the fact was that there I was, mid-life crisis or not, and I still fancied the pants off Joe. And more, felt like he was so mature, and that he could see the younger me inside my corporeal carcass, and that he and I were a good match.

Shit, I'm in trouble here.

Anyway, we threw caution to the wind and went and had a drink at the Beach Bar.

'You're off then,' he said, 'and I'll miss you.'

'Me too.' It was hard to look into his eyes without leaping the table there and then. 'It's all a bit weird.'

'Yes.' He held my gaze. 'Izzie, do you have to go?'

Damn it, that bloody question that had been going round my head all day, he didn't have to say it.

'Joe, I have a life in England, I have a husband and a family. I can't possibly stay here. What on earth would I do?'

'I could think of one or two things.' His smile was lascivious.

'Joe, I can't. My brain's all over the place, and my emotions are up and down like the proverbial prostitute's knickers.'

My resort to humour belied my turmoil. Someone said hello to me, and I realised it was Thornton's Jean, smiling away as ever, just passing by, making small talk. Then asking me if I was alright, which I wished she hadn't, because I thought I was and then the minute someone was nice to me I wanted to bawl my eyes out.

'How's Henry?' she asked.

'Henry? Oh, he's great. Henry's good with colours.'

She looked puzzled, asked me to send him her best, kissed me on both cheeks, shrugged and continued on her way, looking as if all was well in her world.

'Bit caustic, that.' Joe raised an eyebrow. 'Vlad?'

We drank and talked for about an hour, I suppose, and Joe told me how special I was, had enriched his life, that sort of thing. I felt giddy. Even contemplating what could have been with me and Joe played havoc with my molecules. When we left, we found ourselves holding hands. Then back up the cliff top, along the path, and the inevitable lovemaking. Shag. Fornication. Screw. Goodness knows what it was, but it was bloody good.

And then he brought me home, here, to the villa, hugged me and we said goodbye.

It's been a bit of a wrench.

Henry informed me that Mother phoned, she was off on her cruise and had wanted to say goodbye.

Tart. Where did she get it from?

Good on Attila, she'd found that soft centre good and proper. I was sure her oil rig worker, freshly purloined from the OU summer school, was in for a right old time with her. He wouldn't know what had hit him.

I'm having a fag. Okay, my birthday's gone and I've given up, but there just happened to be one lying around, and I can't do deprivation just now. Though I have to say the pleasure of the suck is mingled a bit with the revolting smell that I'm now so conscious of.

More turmoil.

Henry has just surprised me yet again by opening champagne, the last bottle apparently, so I'm off to share a bit with him. It was a great thought, bringing me here, and I do love him for it. I'm girding my loins, ready for the off, and we deserve a quiet little ruminate together before it's all over.

I've packed my bags. In a bit, I'll end the day with a long soak. I've aged here, this month, yet I've got a new lease of life. I shall slap on the Clarins, and give myself a good old exfoliate, scrubbing off the old dead cells, making room for the new, as usual. I shall scrub my body with a body brush, in the relentless battle with cellulite, a perfectly natural body covering that we spend a fortune on trying to discourage.

And then I shall sleep my last sleep under the sky of a million stars.

Faro airport

april 30th 2010

If I thought that seeing Rosemary Connolly was a funny thing happening to me on the way to the Algarve, I have to report an even funnier thing happened to me on the way back.

Last night's champagne loosened our tongues, but not really our brains or our hearts. I had indulged in the long awaited soak that seemed to wash away the dead cells of my soul and rehydrate me as much as was possible for now. We then toasted each other, talked about work, things our house needed doing, all sorts. Henry had put Vlad to bed, so to speak, the previous night, so both our skeletons were firmly locked in their appropriate cupboards.

Or closets.

We'd gone to bed with ourselves in between us, hands touching gently as we each drifted into our dreams. We rose amicably, had fresh orange juice, rinsed the glasses and took one last turn out on the patio. I raised my arms to salute the sun, Henry puffed up his chest.

'Thanks you for an amazing month.' I kissed him on both cheeks, Portuguese style, then we loaded our bags into the car and set off on the journey to Faro.

It was like that day a month ago in reverse. We passed donkeys and wagons, pottery shops, men in silly little toytown trucks, their dogs with tongues drooling in the back. Neither of us pointed and exclaimed this time, just lightly touched hands between the two front seats.

We arrived at the *aeroporto* in good time, and quickly found our check in queue. We stood there, Henry and I, intimate strangers, making ridiculous conversation, an exchange of empty words which were heavy with subtext.

'I hope we're not overweight,' I said.

'Izzie, you're not still worrying about weight are you, being a F-fattist again?'

'No, Henry.' I didn't smile. 'I mean as in do we have too much baggage.'

'I shouldn't think so,' said Henry, 'after all, it was fine on the way out, and we haven't really added much while we were here.'

I felt uncomfortable, polite, evasive.

We probably looked like we were standing and talking like all the other tourists on the line, yet it was as if we had our whole lives jumping up and down inside our skins, filtering out any real connection with each other, or our fellow passengers in the line, who were yakking away in their Midland accents.

'Yow alroight, bab.' A big broiled looking woman shouted to another.

'Fab! Ain' it bin a luvly week though, ey? Don' know if we'll come ere again, our David loved it, didn't ya bab? Not sure if it's roight for me an' Alun, loik, a bit quoi-et for us, know warrImean?'

A Portuguese family stood in front of us. They comprised a well-turned-out woman with tasteful gold jewellery, tight jeans, leather boots; her husband, I presumed, was wearing tailored jeans, a white shirt, a smart black leather jacket. They had with them two children, about four and two, beautiful bambino eyes, dark curly hair adorning angelic faces. I saw them exchange glances. Maybe they were wondering how they would ever get to grips with this strange English language.

So was I.

And then Henry said, 'You know Izzie, it's been a bit of a strange month, and to be honest, I'm just looking forward to going back to work, and getting back to how things used to be.'

A shiver ran through my heart. *How things used to be.* I wasn't sure I wanted that. I remember that *how things used to be* were quite boring actually. More teaching and training, organising family get-togethers from time to time, going out with my friends, planning the next holiday, supporting Henry at work, and sorting out his parents. The prospect of going back to how things used to be seemed about as inspiring as a wet lettuce.

Poor old Henry, he didn't know what hit him. Suddenly, I knew what I had to do. I looked him in the eyes.

'I'm sorry,' I said, 'I can't do this. I love you very much, Henry, but right now I just can't come back with you.'

I picked up my case, leaned forward and gave him a half-hearted hug.

'Izzie, what are you doing?' Henry sounded totally bewildered.

He took hold of my arm.

'Izzie, we can work this out. I can have some counselling. *We* could have some counselling, go to Relate or something.'

Sadly for Henry, the thought of unpicking all our murky emotions, thoughts and deeds just nailed my decision on for me.

'Sorry, Henry, I can't explain right now but I have to go. I'll call you.' I was beginning to walk away. It was then or never.

'But Izzie, what will you do? Fff... '

I have no idea what that last word was going to be. I know I was gathering pace. What was I going to do? No idea. Maybe I'd run a bloody donkey Sanctuary, or work with the local orphans, or lie and get very drunk very often until my money ran out.

By the time I reached the *saida*, the exit, I was running, dragging my big case behind me, which seemed to be as light as a feather. I burst out into the scorching air, ran to the nearest taxi and got myself into it as quickly as possible. I ordered it back to the villa because I didn't know what else to do. I didn't really have a plan.

When I got here, the villa was busy with cleaners. Of course: it would be. There were three of them, all of whom I recognised from when they'd changed towels and such over the month, and they looked at me in surprise.

'*Senhora*.' The oldest of the three women, Portuguese, short and squat, Maria, looked surprised to see me, and slightly panicky. 'You cannot come, we clean.'

A taller, slimmer woman with an eastern European accent was more helpful.

'Vesner?' I tentatively spoke the name, hoping I'd remembered it right.

'Are you all right, lady?' she asked me. 'You are very red in face. Come, you sit down, is all right.'

She fetched me water, which I drank thankfully.

'I am fine. I need to stay here. Cannot go home.' She nodded, sagely.

'Husband?'

I shook my head.

'Ah, very good,' she said, and went back to the kitchen, reappearing with a large glass of wine, and winked at me.

'You are lady alone now, you need somewhere to stay, yes?' and with one or two phone calls, she seems to have found me an apartment for the foreseeable future.

'Is near village. I show you when we finish house. Is on edge of village, will be very nice.'

I nodded, grateful, and sat outside with my wine while they finished the cleaning.

So now I'm ensconced in a small apartment in a fishing village in Portugal, at the end of the most surreal moment of my life. I've just had a large chicken piri-piri takeaway with chips, and have undone the top button of my trousers, bliss.

I look around me, my suitcase parked on the floor, laptop on the table, which is a monstrous dark wood piece with matching monstrous dark sideboard behind it, another glass of wine in hand. I feel older, wiser, freer, than I ever have.

I'm not going back. There is no going back, there is only forwards. But I didn't know this until I was in the airport with Henry, about to check in. Back can't possibly be a part of my future, even if I don't know what can.

I will unpack properly tomorrow, for now I have everything I need in front of me, and my own good self.

I have texted Henry just to let him know that I am safe and well and have said that I will be in touch when I know what I'm doing. Now my phone is switched off.

I've no idea what will happen next, and to be honest with you, I don't bloody care. Well I do, but not in the sense of worrying about it. I am, after all, the woman who was determined not to have a mid-life crisis☺. I've every confidence that I shall not only be happy here but that I'll find something which has been eluding me for quite some time. I'm not sure what shape or form it will take.

There's a knock on the door, which is weird, because nobody knows I'm here.

'*Momento! Um momento!*'

Portuguese. I said it in Portuguese. See, it'll be easy.

Acknowledgements

My affair with the Algarve began in 1991, on a pilgrimage to meet an independent young woman, named Sam Watson. Sam fielded magnificently that first visit from me, her *madrasta bruxa*, her dad, the siblings, and dear Aunty Gladbags, who never travelled without the best of intentions and the biggest of wooden spoons. I can't say it went without a hitch.

Now, I am blessed with our next cosmopolitan generation, Rebeca, Andre, Joseph and Lilliana, all here because of meetings in Portugal. I thank my lucky stars and Sam: if you'd not been there, my affair with the Algarve, and all else besides, might never have begun. Your knowledge of the region is immense, your generosity endless, introducing me to people, parties, places, the concept of the never-ending meal at Fernanda's; the Women's Business Network. You are a star, a daughter and a friend.

While I was President of the Algarve Women's Network, I ran a short story competition, and met Lisa Selvidge, now my editor, publisher, and *amiga*. I have laughed and learned from sessions of workshopping and co-scripting with you. Don't mention the *medronho*☺. You remind me that my writing needs to be hung on a wall, just as one would any other piece of art. You are an extraordinary woman, incisive critic, and an inspiring writer.

Suzi Steinhofel designed the cover for the book. I met Suzi through the Women's Network, she wore pink suede boots. Suzi, you are generous, savvy, and creative. Thank you for much that you have given me, quite apart from the cover design. Keep on making life great, and laughing your wonderful laugh.

As ever, I would like to acknowledge those who personally support my work with belief, encouragement and feedback, some reading it over and over again, especially Graham, Keziah, Sara, and Sue. One day I hope Samuel will get to read one of my works from cover to cover, as I would love to hear the verdict.

As for the stories in the book, well, they are down to my imagination, my misspent youth, my complicated adulthood, and many hilarious night chats with friends.

I would like finally to acknowledge Doris Trott for being the teacher who let me know I really could write, and more importantly, that I was equal to the other girls, even though I was the only one in the second-hand blazer. Thank you.

16972515R00109

Printed in Great Britain
by Amazon